QUINLAN'S LAW

A Promise To Keep

DARREL SPARKMAN

A Dedication:

To my wife Sue who catches most of my mistakes.
She obviously listened in school.

~ * ~ * ~ * ~

Heartfelt Thanks:

Linda Broday, Author
Tonya Lucas, Reviewer
For invaluable insight and honest feedback.

~ * ~ * ~ * ~

*From such a talented author,
Darrel Sparkman delivers an ending
that had me gasping and cringing. I highly recommend this
explosive western to anyone who thrives on action,
romance, and seeing evil eradicated.*

— Review by Tonya Lucas

ೞ*ೞ

QUINLAN'S LAW
A Promise To Keep

1879 was a year of endless summer. In the wind-swept grasslands of eastern Kansas, dust storms moved more dirt than German farmers.

Quinlan Barrett called himself lucky. Unscathed from a gunfight with rustlers, he was ready to call it quits and try something new. Falling under the spell of beautiful ranch girl Consuela Pinder was a start. But then she was abducted by the madman Macrae, uncovering a group of slavers selling women into old Mexico.

Since leaving the hills of northern Arkansas, Quinlan Barrett always wore a badge. Deputy US Marshal in Indian Territory, railroad detective on the KATY, and then livestock inspector out of the Kansas City Stockyards. He still carried a badge, but it was deep in his pocket.

Aided by the scout Kiowa Smith, Exoduster Zeke Fontenot, and a few remnants of the old Cherokee Brigade, Quin sets out to do the two things he was good at.

There was killing to do and promises to keep.

CONTENTS

A Promise To Keep

Chapter One

The night is swiftly passing,
the battle is on the morn.
An old man is a pitiful thing indeed.

~ Walk With Peril by D.V.S Jackson

It was an odd day. He'd read stories about the great deserts in far off places where the wind moved sand like waves across an ocean. This couldn't be much different. The midday sun was a hazy ring, and at ground level darkness over-powered the light. Periodically the wind would stop, the dust settle, and the merciless sun would scorch everything beneath it. Then the cycle would start again. It was an endless battle played out on the prairies of Kansas between sun, wind, and dust—all forces of nature intent on crushing life between them.

The earth was parched and desperate for rain and if it didn't happen soon there wouldn't be enough dirt left to grow prickly pear, much less grass for livestock. All the usable soil would be scattered from Missouri to Nebraska—except for what he could beat out of his clothes. His shirt alone might be worth a fortune to some desperate farmer. If he could summon the moisture to spit, it would dry up before striking the ground.

Quinlan Barrett eased himself in the saddle, head lowered against the wind. Every nook and cranny of his body seemed full of dirt. He could barely see as he leaned into the wind and tightened his faded, blue-checked bandanna over his nose and below his eyes. He'd tied his hat down with a strip of leather fished from his saddlebag, so his view of the world around him was narrow. He hated traveling blind. Surprised by how quickly the wind rose, he was looking for a sheltered place to make a miserable camp.

West of Kansas City and north of Emporia, he was returning after checking a couple of herds being driven toward the stockyards. He took his job as livestock inspector seriously, moving from ranch to homestead checking livestock for altered brands.

He gave up telling himself the weather was dry, conceding to the boredom of the day that he'd run out of eloquent description of circumstance. Quin was about to turn his back to the wind and take his chances when the faint lowing of cattle came to him, surprising since his ears were full of dirt. It was curious because he knew a trail herd was a few miles behind him, but nothing was close by.

Topping a rise, a small mixed herd of cattle shuffled stoically with their tails to the wind in the shallow valley below. If the wind didn't let up soon the cattle would start drifting, but that wasn't his problem. He was curious about why these cattle were bunched up. They wouldn't do that on their own unless they ran into a fence or bluff they couldn't climb.

Several men hunched in the windbreak of a rock outcropping, surrounded by brush and huddled around a fire that sported a large coffee pot hung on a metal tripod like you'd see in most cow camps. The contents of that pot had to be half mud by now.

These men didn't look like drovers. Even from a distance and through the veneer of dust he could see their clothing looked too new, the colors weren't faded and he could see the gleam off a fancy gun belt or two. Riders rarely wore anything shiny that might spook cattle, couldn't afford such finery anyway.

Directly behind the camp, the real mystery was swaying in the wind gusts with three-part harmony of hemp sawing in loose knots, wearing through the bark of a convenient tree limb. Three bodies hung by their necks from ropes. Murder or retribution? This part of the country was fed up with rustling. Lately, the dust storms made things easy for rustlers and hard for anyone trying to find them. But which were these men? Saints or sinners?

Flipping the loops off his pistols and pulling back the curved hammers on the Greener, he moved Red down the slope. The horse knew something was up, because he stepped light through the scattered rock and prickly pear cactus. He and Red had been through a lot and he often thought the horse could read his mind.

When the fickle Kansas wind stopped blowing, Quin must have appeared to the men like a ghost dancer appearing from a smoky fire. The temperature probably rose twenty degrees the moment he appeared. Sweat would be making muddy streams soon and those bodies hanging from the tree were going to get ripe.

With a startled oath, one of the men stood abruptly, reaching for his pistol. Quin unleashed one barrel of his coach gun into their campfire. That ten-gauge shotgun was not kind to whatever it hit. Sparks flew into the air when the 00 buckshot hit rocks and the coffee pot broke loose and slammed into the ashes. It was a jarring sound in the absence of wind.

Quin spoke in a reasonable voice, strained by dust, dearly needing a drink of water. "I'd appreciate it if you boys would just settle down and sit still."

There were four men and two half-grown boys staring at him with mouths open and eyes wide. The pot lay on its side, ripped open and leaking sludge. One of their horses broke loose from its tether, and then stood confused, wild-eyed and snorting.

"You," Quin pointed to the man who'd made a try for his pistol, a man with so much curly hair he'd have to nail his hat down with spikes. "I'm a reasonable man on occasion. Please explain those tree ornaments to me."

Curly looked nervously at his partners. "You want us to throw our pistols away?"

"You don't seem to follow directions well." That was a curious question from the man if they were innocent, so he shrugged. "Not now."

"Who the hell are you?" The dust was starting to kick up again, so he didn't see who spoke. That double-barreled shotgun was heavy, so it took some doing to hold it steady while digging out his badge holder and hanging it on his vest pocket with his other hand.

"My name is Quinlan Barrett. I'm a livestock investigator out of Kansas City." Quin immediately steadied the Greener with both hands.

The belligerent response from Curly was immediate. "In other words, you're nobody."

Quin shrugged and gave a rueful smile. "My folks would be upset to hear that, but it's a fair description. You still haven't answered the question."

Curly stood slow, keeping his hands away from his sides, his gaze flicking side-to-side apparently looking for other threats. "For your information Mister Investigator, those men were rustlers. They got what they deserved. Now, why don't you ride on out of here and let us be? This is none of your concern." He gave a cold smile. "If you don't, we got room for one more on that tree. Of course, we're fresh out of rope...we'd have to use yours."

"Stop right there." Quin's voice rapped out. The men next to the loudmouth Curly were getting restless and a couple started to rise. "I told you once to sit still. Next time I'll shoot anyone who moves."

Curly had been standing with hands half-raised. He dropped his arms to put his hands on his hips and blustered. "You got no right to...."

"Get your hands up and away from that pistol." Quin warned. He cursed himself for getting into this mess. It was getting out of hand in a hurry. Anytime you have to warn someone, you've already lost. "How do you know those men were rustlers?"

"Easy." Curly had a greasy grin that never reached his eyes. "They had cattle that didn't belong to them." His smile grew large for a moment before he continued. "You're all by yourself, aren't you?"

"Yessir. It's just me. Why? Am I supposed to feel surrounded? Outnumbered by y'all?" Quin gave the man a hard look. "This ain't the Greasy Grass and you aren't Crazy Horse."

Quin considered himself a friendly sort and liked to hear a good story, if told well. If there was a punch line to this one, they weren't selling it. The man's bluster was starting to wear thin. "Now, suppose you tell me how you know these cattle were stolen?"

Curly shrugged, glancing at the other men. "We're with the J-Bar trail herd that's a few miles southwest of here and we've been chasing these men for a couple of days."

Cattle inspectors have to know brands, it was part of the job. The J-Bar was one he'd seen. It was also a brand that could be altered to about any other brand. Stupidity wears many suits, and if a ranch owner wants a brand that anyone with a running iron could alter? That was on him.

"Alright." Quin pointed to one of the youngsters. "Bring me one of your horses. If the brand is right, we'll leave things as they are and I'll be on my way. If not, I'll be taking all of you in for murder."

"You got no authority to do that." Another of the men was starting to get to his feet, only to settle back down when the barrel of Quin's shotgun pointed at him.

"You can argue that with the judge. We'll call it a citizen's arrest." Quin shrugged. "Hell boys, you might get off scot free. Most of the judges don't like me, so they'll probably take your side and buy you a steak dinner."

"This is crazy." The man shook his head. "There's six of us and one of you. You don't have a chance."

"I wasn't aware I'd need a chance since you claim to be on the up-and-up. But if it comes down to it, you call the tune and I'll dance to it." On a hot and dusty day like this Quin wouldn't have to worry about slippery palms when drawing a weapon. He was getting an itchy feeling between his shoulders. Then to add to the first mistake of riding into this situation in the first place he made a second mistake, turning to see where that kid had gone.

Chapter Two

Seeing Quin distracted, the men around the fire went for their guns. Bunched up as they were, they got in each other's way trying to scramble to their feet, bumping elbows and cussing each other in their haste to get off a shot. One man tripped on a blanket and fell into the fire. His screaming added to the confusion.

Funny thing about that double-barrel shotgun. The left barrel he'd used on the coffeepot was full choke, so the pattern was tight. The right barrel had no constriction at all, that's why they called it a scattergun.

When they all moved at once Quin was startled. With a curse he pulled the trigger and then dropped the shotgun by its sling over the saddle horn. In the same motion, he drew his belly gun and started shooting. He didn't remember sliding off his horse and switching to his side gun but it was surely in his hand at the end.

The shotgun did its work if nothing more than sowing discontent and confusion. That double-aught buckshot hurts, but then so does a forty-four-caliber lead ball.

The wind cleared out the gun smoke to find Quin standing behind his horse with four men down before him. Breathing as if he'd run a mile, he did a quick check and found he was free of wounds. That was a miracle. He knew that in the heat of battle, sometimes a wound was scarcely felt until later.

Red stood rigid, eyes distended and blowing air in gusts from his nostrils. Quin's last few shots had been from under Red's neck. He took a moment to calm the horse before stepping around him.

The youngster sitting by the fire hadn't moved, so he didn't get shot. The other stood off to the side with his mouth open, holding a horse's reins. Quin paused a moment, feeding shells into his pistols. His belly gun was a short-barreled Colt and his side gun was a hand cannon—the number three Schofield.

He could see why the boy didn't approach, because the brand on the horse didn't match the cattle. You'd think he would have found one of the drover's horses to bring that would have matched, but the boy was scared and didn't appear too bright in the first place. This probably wasn't how the boy thought his day would go. It was a communal thought.

~ * ~

It took a while, but he got it sorted out. Like he suspected, the poor souls hanging from that tree were innocent drovers from the herd, just looking for strays. The honest cowhands somehow let the rustlers disarm them and then got hung for their mistake. If there was ever an argument for never giving up your guns, this was it. When he cut the men down he could see the bodies were used for target practice. That was an assumption. It made little sense to shoot them and then hang them later, especially given the difficulty of moving a dead body. Judging from the number of holes, it was a wonder the rustlers had any ammunition left.

Finished with laying out the cowhands, he watched the boys a moment, thinking it over. "Where are you boys from?"

One was sniffling and wiping his nose on the sleeve of his shirt, and the other stared glumly at the ground. They looked similar, towheaded and blue-eyed, neither old enough to start a beard. He figured they were brothers.

"We got a place west of here. Over past Honey Creek a few miles." The boy answering the question never raised his gaze from his feet.

"Why'd you steal these cattle?" Quin asked.

The older brother snapped his head up. "That trail herd drove right over our gardens, broke our fences down and scattered our livestock all over hell and gone. We lost our milk cows...everything. They even knocked over our barn." He motioned toward the drovers, laid out in a line. "When Ma asked them to pay for the damages, all they did was laugh about it. They said free range didn't need no farmers."

It surely couldn't be much of a barn, but Quin had seen a few ramshackle things put together that it could happen to. Poor folks used what they had to get by. It wasn't a new story, but something that happened time to time. To drive cattle to market, ranchers needed room. Farmers moved into fertile land under the Homestead Act of 1862 for their free 160 acres, often fencing off their sections in a valley the drovers might use to get the cattle between the hills—a matter of logistics. It was a dilemma where both sides were right, and both were wrong.

Quin asked. "Did you see all that happen?"

The boy shook his head. "Naw. We'd been fishing the creek for supper. The mudcats were biting. We could hear the cattle, but didn't think too much about it." He chin-pointed toward the pile of dead rustlers. "These men come up later, offered to help. We went along with them, figured it was our duty."

"Next time someone offers to help, take a long look at why they're doing it. I think you can see these men were looking for an opportunity to steal cattle." Quin's shoulders slumped as he watched them. He'd just killed four men in front of them and it looked as if his words of wisdom were falling on deaf ears. But then, at their age he knew everything too. It takes a while to learn that you're born stupid and it just gets worse from there. With a little luck and perseverance, knowledge grows.

It was quiet for once. The wind stopped trying to uproot every plant and tree, a wren fussed in the brush. He stared around the small clearing, shaking his head slowly. Nothing was ever simple.

Quin addressed the older brother. "You're ma alone right now?"

"Just her and the young ones." The boy's answer was despondent.

"How about your pa?" Quin asked. The boys were painting a picture he didn't like. A woman alone on a beat-down homestead with kids to take care of. If this were one of those adventure books, he'd be riding to the rescue. That wasn't a road he wanted to travel.

"Horse rolled over Pa a couple years back. We been making do." The boy was back to looking at the ground when he answered, scuffing dirt with the worn-out toe of his homemade boot.

If Quin took these boys to Kansas City, they'd be hung for the sins of their elders—guilt by association. He figured the rustlers saw it as an easy way to cut a few head out of the herd, under cover of the bad weather and the guise of retribution. The boys just went along to represent the family, probably as a respite from fishing for mudcat. It was an adventure seated in bad decisions and ending in gun smoke.

After collecting what papers there were from the drovers for identification, he put the boys to digging three graves. Most every westerner carried a small shovel for digging a fire pit, at least in dry country. They found a couple in the packs.

"Why not seven graves?" The younger brother finally spoke, wiping away muddy tears.

"These rustlers don't deserve to be buried," Quin replied, hoping it was another lesson for them. "The buzzards and coyotes can have them."

When they finished the sun was just past its apex. If they weren't close to sun stroke, it was next on their list of things to do. He let the boys keep their pistols and gifted them a couple of beat-up Henry rifles for their saddles. They hadn't thought to bring water, so he gave them a couple of canteens which they promptly emptied. Everything else was wrapped in blankets to drape over one of the horses. Rifles were tied together and pistol belts hung over saddle horns.

Quin's saddle had a bullet crease and a splintered the pommel, so he swapped it for another saddle that was bought with more money than he made in a month and put it on one of the rustler's horses—a black gelding with a skittish look to him. From the marks on his flanks, the horse had been abused some. If the horse didn't kill him first, maybe he'd gentle down. He would do to ride until Red healed.

Red had a bullet hole in his neck, just under the mane. Counting the two holes in Quin's saddle, one which made it through and barely broke the skin on the horse's side. That was three bullets that missed his lucky carcass. If he were Catholic, he'd be lighting candles at the next church he came to—he might anyway.

He was grateful those men couldn't shoot well. Quin apologized to his horse several times while applying liniment for infection and Red stomped on his foot. After dealing out that indignity and watching Quin jump around on one foot for a minute, the horse seemed satisfied.

The cattle had spooked from the gunfire, but the wind would drive them back toward their own herd. Quin figured he'd follow along so he could report to the herd boss what had happened and where to find his men.

They'd done everything needed for the moment and he stood in front of the boys. They hadn't said much after the burying, just providing what names of the rustlers that they knew. The drovers had enough papers on them to supply their names. Quin wrote it all out in his journal and then had the boys sign it. The events of gun smoke and death had been reduced to a list on paper, stowed in his saddlebag.

There was a lot that didn't sound right about the whole deal, but Quin was too weary to figure it out. One thing was sure. These young men were surrounded by a lot of misfortune.

"Boys, here's the way it's gonna be. I didn't look at your names when you signed that paper. I don't want to know who you are. I don't want to know who your mother is. I don't want to know where you came from. As far as I'm concerned, you dropped out of the sky and left the same way. You boys grab your horses, take whatever supplies you need, and get on back home. Take care of your mother and the young ones. Take care of your farm. No more stealing, you can see where that leads."

They stood looking at him, mouths open in astonishment. He was beginning to think that was a family trait.

"Well?" He pointed west. "Go."

He watched them leave before mounting his new, borrowed horse. All the extra gear was tied to the rustler's horses, and all the horses were on a tail-to-hackamore string. The saddles were tightened just enough so they wouldn't fall off. He didn't think the herd was far away.

The herd boss would just add all the extra horses to their remuda. Quin would let them sort out notifying the families of the dead men. That was a common occurrence on a trail drive.

There was only about forty dollars in the pockets of the miscreants. He didn't know how that would be split up. The amount would go in his report and then he'd turn it over to the owner of the trail herd. His best hope was to not get shot delivering all of it.

Turning in the saddle, he looked back at the little valley dominated by a sycamore with low branches. It was better to be lucky than good on any day, and he'd ridden into a risky situation. It would have been better to hang back and figure out what was going on...maybe go to the trail herd for reinforcements. That would have been the smart play. Although he tried hard, being smart was elusive.

On their part, the rustlers were in too big of a hurry to kill him, jumping up from a sitting position and shooting while trying to find cover for themselves. He was lucky Red was a good horse that stood steady, even when he was shot. Again. Better lucky than good.

It was a once-in-a-lifetime deal that he came out alive, defying any rational thought, and he didn't want to push his luck anymore.

Looking at the shallow graves, and four bodies in violent repose, it took longer than it should have to realize he was done with this job. Sighing, he put his back to the wind and drifted behind the stolen cattle.

Chapter Three

Following the small, rustled herd of cattle gave Quin time to reflect. It was easy to look back and see mistakes...harder still to look forward with any level of prediction. His parents were well read and sent him into the world educated better than most, ready to make good decisions. That's no guarantee you make them.

The Civil War hadn't touched his family much. Their place was on a high plateau, a grassy plain of several hundred acres in northern Arkansas. They didn't want for much, raising all they needed for food and trade. Trips to places like Joplin to the north, and Fayetteville to the south were infrequent. His parents had been schoolteachers before retiring at a young age to their mountain abode. The important thing was that access to their place was limited to one easily defended trail—defended against the North and South alike. The occasional curious patrols were discouraged easily, the dislike for visitors was bipartisan and soon spread.

Fresh out of the rolling hills, Quin was recruited as a Deputy US Marshal working out of Fort Smith and into Indian Territory by Judge Isaac Parker. His only qualification for that job was that a deputy saw him win several shooting matches for walking around money. It was a job he should have turned down. But being well educated in numbers and verse didn't mean he was smart, or knew the way of the world. Young and impetuous, he asked the judge why he hung so many men. The judge had replied, "I don't hang them, the law does."

Quin read in the local newspaper that the judge didn't believe in capital punishment, but seemed to distribute it freely. It was a mystery founded in disbelief for most folks.

What Quin should have understood was that the US Marshal for that district, never leaving his office during the workday, was paid ninety dollars a month. The deputy marshals were paid two dollars for delivering a summons, or bringing in the evildoer, plus six cents a mile in performance of their duty. Occasionally a reward was paid by the railroad for the apprehension of a criminal, but often that money would go to the marshal's office. If Quin hadn't brought firearms and his own horse from his home in Arkansas, he wouldn't have been able to afford them.

When he began the job, Quin thought being a deputy would garner respect from his fellow man. It did not. There was no glamor in man hunting. It was a dirty job. Especially since most men deserving a warrant and knowing the reputation of the judge in Fort Smith, would much rather die by a bullet than a hangman's noose. They never came willingly.

He'd been shot at, spit at and cussed at more than any job he'd ever had in his short life—excepting maybe that whore house in Joplin that the city marshal finally closed because they wouldn't pay their fee. Everything in Joplin was legal, for a fee.

Judge Parker must have had badges made by the hundred. He gave them away like candy, and most came back with blood on them. If they came back.

He had to smile at the memories, trying to watch the hills around him and wary of an ambush. A broke cow pusher and sometime farmer from the hills of Arkansas will do some stupid things for a twenty-dollar gold piece. The pay for bringing in someone for trial might get him two dollars, plus six dollars in mileage—provided he could ride in circles for fifty miles. He used a large day book, wrapped in leather, to keep his journal and figure all his high finances.

Quitting the marshal's service and riding the KATY railroad from Fort Smith to Kansas City, he'd been offered a job as railroad detective. His qualification for that job was not being able to mind his own business. Quin had intervened when a couple of drunk and unruly roughnecks tried to throw the conductor off the train. The train wasn't moving too fast, but the fall would still have left the poor man bruised up—maybe dead. Still, thinking back on it, he should have minded his own business.

The new railroad badge was just as shiny as the last, but carried less weight. He couldn't arrest anyone, but no one cared how he adjudicated the rules of the railroad or listened to the complaints of those who received punishment.

After working that job awhile, he went against his better judgment and bellied up to a table in one of the finer KC hotel restaurants. He had money to spend and would rather feed himself than give it to someone in a local game of chance—gambling is never left to chance. He wasn't much of a detective, because when a man offered to buy his steak, it should have been his clue to leave. A new entry in his journal should have been that nothing is done for nothing.

Talk of money was flowing freely, along with a couple of brands of skull-buster. He let Thaddeus Finch, the head of The Kansas City Livestock Association, convince him to earn some of it. After all, the railroad just paid a salary. This new job paid salary plus commission, a large amount of money for such an easy job. But money was what he needed if he wanted his own ranch someday. And the more he thought of it, that was exactly what he wanted.

All he was supposed to do was find out who rustled cattle from the herds coming into the KC stockyards. The day of the huge cattle drive was gone, but some local ranchers still drove their cattle to market. Quin's job was to bird-dog the miscreants and give the stockyard folks a heads-up on the pilfered cattle or changed brands. The Association would take care of the rest. Easy money.

~ * ~

It took Quin less than an hour to find the herd. The drovers had stopped trying to drive the cattle into the wind, and were keeping them bunched up—or trying to. Between the wind and dust, the confused and thirsty cattle were sneaking into every ravine and draw they passed.

Seeing Quin following cattle toward their camp, most of the men of the J-Bar didn't waste any time cutting them off. Hands on the pommel of his saddle, Quin waited. He didn't neglect to take the thongs off his pistols and make sure the Greener was loaded.

Within minutes the curious riders were stretched in a line before him, about fifteen strong with more on the way. One of the men broke ranks and rode the length of his little caravan, taking time eye-balling the J-Bar horses, and then came back to sit in front of him. They were close enough that Quin was surprised his horse didn't take a bite out of something.

The rider's voice was rough. "Reckon you got some explaining to do."

Quin had left the Livestock Association badge pinned to his vest hoping that would at least give him time to explain. He had no intention of being intimidated. "And you might be?"

The man answered like his name should mean something. Since Quin led a somewhat sheltered life in limited social circles, it did not. "My name's Walter Pike. I'm the trail boss for this outfit."

Nodding in acknowledgment, Quin said. "Well, Mister Pike. I'm Quinlan Barrett, out of Kansas City. I found some of your cattle back yonder. I also found the owners of those J-Bar horses hanging from a sycamore tree. Can you read, sir?"

"What the hell...?" The man colored up some, thrown off by the direct approach. "I can."

Quin reached into his saddlebag for his leather-wrapped day book, hearing several pistols cock when he made the sudden movement. Most revolvers went through a double or even a triple click to be ready to fire. It sounded like he'd stepped in a nest of mouse traps all set off at once.

"Mister Pike, please inform your men that I get unpredictable when guns are pointed at me. You'd do to remember that. Now, here's the report I'm filing with the Livestock Association, and the US Marshal in Kansas City. It'll save us from talking against the wind and losing our voices if you just read it."

Quin handed over the journal, watching pistols disappear into holsters, and waited while the trail boss worked his way through the report. The riders on each side of the man tried to see what Pike was reading.

Finally, Pike handed it back. "Your chicken scratching could use some work."

"I've heard that." Quin nodded. "My teachers were some disappointed in my efforts."

The trail boss continued. "You killed four men? I wouldn't believe that hearing it from anyone else. But I've heard your name spoken, time to time. Not in a good way. I thought you were down in the Nation bringing in people for the judge to hang."

Before Quin could answer, Pike turned to his men. "Take these horses, strip them, and turn them into the remuda. The rest of the tack and belongings can go to the possibles wagon to be sorted through later."

Quin shouted at them over the wind. "Leave the sorrel with the shot-up saddle. He's mine."

After nodding his OK to the men, Pike turned to him. Taking off his hat and wiping the sweat band, he asked. "About how far back would our men be?"

Shrugging, Quin said. "An hour, give or take. Your cattle left a pretty good trail. It should still be there, even in this wind. We buried the men shallow, in case you wanted to move them. They're wrapped in blankets."

Pike nodded acceptance, settling his hat firmly on his head. "And those rustlers?"

"Attracting buzzards." Quin replied. "We didn't waste any time with them and left them where they lay."

"Alright." The man turned in the saddle, addressing the few men left. "Russell, you take a few men and see to the boys. Just make sure they're buried good, maybe some rocks on top, with markers. That's about all we can do for them."

When Pike finished issuing orders, he turned back to Quin. "That shot-up saddle on the sorrel. You say that's yours?"

Glancing at Red, he replied. "It is."

The trail boss snorted. "Might have been smarter for you to bushwhack them. As it was, it was a good thing you vacated that saddle when the shooting started."

"Maybe." It was an opinion Quin shared. "The problem was, I couldn't tell the saints from the sinners until I talked to them. I had a suspicion, but even then I didn't really know for sure how things were until they pulled iron. Once that happened, it was a little late to plan a good campaign."

Pike chuckled, leaning with his rough hands on the pommel. "And those two boys you let go. You sure about that?"

"No. With something like that you're never sure. It was a judgment call and today's judgment is sometimes tomorrow's disaster." He pinned the man with a level gaze. "They did have an interesting story to tell. I'm thinking you should know those boys. The way they told it, you drove roughshod over their place and disrespected their mother—tore up their gardens and tore down fences. That sound about right?"

Pike sat straight in the saddle, tense for a moment before answering. "It's no wonder you're good with a gun. You rub a man raw."

"Alright, that's two things I need to work on. Handwriting skills and personality. I'll keep that in mind." Quin continued. "Next time I pass this way, I'll visit their place...maybe check on the family. I have a good idea where the homestead is. What I want to hear from the boy's mother you disrespected is how generous you were about replacing what your herd destroyed, and how sincere your apology was. You have enough men with you that it wouldn't take half a day of honest work to make it right."

Pike shook his head, turning and spitting with the wind. "My drovers fixing up a shoddy farm. It won't happen."

"I'm sure they can make the sacrifice." Quin replied. "If you have some orphan calves, you might donate them—they just slow you down anyway."

New calves weren't really orphans, but the drovers kept the cattle on the move all day. There was no time for momma to stop and nurse. The calves were often carried in the freight, or possibles, wagon, a rare occurrence, or left to die in the wake of the herd as it moved on.

"We don't have time to...." Pike's voice was loud, anger tossed against the wind.

"You should take the time, Mister Pike." Quin replied calmly, hands folded on the pommel of his saddle. "Until this wind lets up, you're just chasing your tails anyway. It'll give your riders something to do."

The man settled in his saddle, glaring at Quin. "I don't like being told what to do and you have no authority to order me around. You're not a marshal anymore."

"You're right on all counts—just trying to point you in the right direction, knowing you're such a good person and upstanding citizen." Quin tipped his hat. "Do the right thing, Mister Pike. That family has heartache enough. You have a good evening, sir. Tell your boys I appreciate their help."

Most homesteaders lived a precarious existence on the prairie. A fair amount of their food was raised in their garden. Having it ruined wasn't an inconvenience like some cattlemen thought. If they lost their milk cows, goats, and chickens to a herd of cattle trampling through, added to a ruined garden? It was life and death.

The trail boss fumed a moment, staring into the distance before pining Quin with an angry gaze. "I'd invite you 'light and set' for the night, belly up to the chuck wagon, but considering...."

"That's alright, Mister Pike. I appreciate the custom, but I need to keep moving." Quin interrupted. "We don't have to like each other to have respect. I wouldn't want to lose that over a few fences and trampled gardens."

After a short salute to his hat brim, he gave a gentle tug to the rope tied to Red's bridle, and turned his horse toward Kansas City. There were decisions to make and plenty of time to ponder them on the trail.

Chapter Four

The two-day trip to Kansas City was uneventful. After selling the black horse from the rustler's remuda, and putting Red in livery, Quin stood before a two-storied brick and mortar building that overlooked the confluence of the Missouri and Kaw rivers. Residents called the area the west bottoms. If he understood the stories right, it had been a miserable place since Chouteau's Landing was put up in 1821, given to floods and mosquitoes large enough to carry off small children.

Kansas City was never his favorite place to be, it was too busy with more people per acre than he cared to count. A week had passed since the shootout with the rustlers. The wind had stopped, the air was clear, and he felt halfway decent. God hadn't struck him down for his sins with a lightning bolt...yet.

There were a couple of good, secluded springs just outside of the city and the one he found was turned into a mud hole after he took a bath and then washed his clothes. If he cried, tears would still be muddy water, but he didn't plan on it. At least, not today. His eyes were still scratchy enough to make him go back on that. He was sure he looked like a red-eyed monster from a child's fable.

He stomped up the steps to the building, which looked like an enormous red brick box. The polished floors reminded him of ice and he wondered how many janitors it took to keep the place pristine. He gingerly made his way to the stairs leading to the second floor. Catching his breath, he was thinking a horse ramp would be appreciated.

The few times he'd met with Finch, his gatekeeper and secretary always sat at a desk placed next to heavy oak doors. Mildred always presented a straight back and suspicious manner as she watched him approach.

Her desk was smooth as the floor, reflecting sunlight from a single window—no clutter, no paper, and certainly no dust, just her hands folded primly on the surface. He wondered if she was simply an ornament like the potted plants and paintings on the wall. Her expression didn't change as he walked by with a nod and tip of his hat. She might be long dead and petrified except her eyes tracked him across the floor.

The cattle business must be good, because the office of Thaddeus Finch, Esquire was larger than most homes found on the prairie. Plants in ornate pots stood in wilted repose next to windows made opaque with dust. No amount of rain would ever clean them.

The leather furniture, and walls made of oak planks, reminded him of the House of Lords in Joplin. That was a place he could barely afford to peek at through the windows, much less visit the doves on the third floor. It was a high dollar establishment frequented mainly by the elite of the mining industry—and monthly by the town marshal to collect fees.

Quin sat in a plush, hard-backed chair while Finch read his report. Finished, the man poured them both a shot of whiskey from an unlabeled bottle and sighed. After toasting to their good health, he got down to business.

"You should have brought in those young boys." Finch finger-tapped the journal and the page opened in front of him.

Contemplating the amber liquid in his heavy glass, Quin replied. "I shouldn't have had to shoot those men in the first place."

Finch was unconcerned, shrugging and looking a little perturbed. "It's not your fault. They were rustlers."

Quin finished off his drink, finally raising his gaze to meet Finch's. "Still...not my job. I should have taken note of the brands and rode away. It was a mistake in judgement."

"That's kind of a gray area, you know that. From what you say in your report, those men were murderers in the worst way." Finch watched him closely. "What else could you do?"

Quin shook his head. "That's not the way it was supposed to be. The deal was that I make a report on the brands and drovers. When they come into the stockyards, you pick up anyone with altered brands and arrest them. Simple. I'm tired of getting shot at."

Finch waved the complaint away with a flick of his wrist. "Speaking of arresting, the marshal dropped by the other day."

"THE marshal?" Quin gave him a curious look. "As in...?"

"US Marshal Gresham himself." Finch tossed a star across the table. "He left this for you and told me not to take no for an answer. You're back on the books as a special investigator, no salary of course. Congratulations, now your shooting of the rustlers was legal."

"Retroactive legality. That's why I hate lawyers." Quin looked at the badge, glowing like a malevolent eye from sunlight filtered through the window. Close inspection showed no indentations or chips from lead balls. "I've no intention in using that. I gave that up, remember?"

"Seems to me you've carried a badge representing law and order since you rode out of Arkansas. It's in your blood." Finch raised a placating hand. "You don't have to serve warrants or anything. It's just for services rendered...and in case you ever need it in the future."

"Now, why would I need...?" A cold knot was forming in Quin's stomach. "You mean, in case you need me."

Finch settled in his chair after pouring himself another shot from the bottle. "There's a business opportunity you could help with since you're wanting to retire. I'm thinking it would help both of us if you could take advantage of it."

Several things were running through Quin's mind, none of them good. He'd once heard an Otoe, down in the Nation, describe confusion as leaping on your horse and riding in all directions. He was settling on the story about a Trojan Horse and bewaring Greeks bringing gifts. In their short relationship, he'd never heard of Finch doing anything for nothing. He doubted the man would start now.

Listening to himself asking the question was like watching himself make mistakes from afar and having no control over it. "What kind of business?"

"There's a nice ranch that can be had for little or nothing. The outbuildings and house were built by a German fella and they're strong as a fortress. I've heard it's quite the place. There's an interesting story to go with it." Finch leaned forward with his arms on the desk, holding the bottle of whiskey.

When Finch refilled his glass, Quin set it on the table, instead of drinking. "How interesting a story...exactly."

"Well," Finch began. "When the surveyors laid out the state line on the north side of the Cherokee Lands in Indian Territory, they got a little drunk. Instead of a straight line, they took the easy way, followed the lay of the land so to speak and jogged north a couple of miles into Kansas. It will be re-surveyed someday and corrected, but for now that little notch into Kansas is technically Indian Territory."

Quin's gaze traced the ornate rolled-tin ceiling, the scroll work etched in shadow from the windows, berating himself for asking. "And the point is...?"

The man grinned. "The point is, Washington is opening Indian Territory for settlement. The legislation is pending, but it will be free land for all under the existing Homestead Act. Someone should snap that place up. You could get an early start and beat the rush."

"That's Indian land. I suspect they won't too be happy about that." Quin knew there were continuous efforts from the bureaucrats in Washington, DC to renege on their treaties with the Indian tribes and open the territory for settlement. To the politicians, all that wide-open land was going to waste. Apparently they hadn't seen western Kansas—it was worse. Of course, the big kicker for settlement was water. Indian Territory had a lot more water than Kansas, especially the eastern parts.

"The Indian question?" Finch flicked imaginary dust from his lapel. "A minor point."

Many of the tribes who resettled by treaty into the land some were calling Oklahoma were still trying to live by the old ways. Quin felt sorry for them. It mostly resulted in them being destitute and mad at everyone around them. You can't take a people that were used to hunting for a living and move them to a land good for farming and ranching. Many refused to be relocated and he didn't blame them.

"I still don't see your point," Quin said. "My sense of it is I should stay away from that land. Most people in that part of the country use deputy marshals, retired or not, for target practice."

"Investigator, not deputy." Finch was shaking his head again. "Here's the thing. I like you, Quin. You're a strong man and can hold what you take. There's a good ranch in that strip of no-man's land. It's called the Spring Valley Ranch, but you can call it Goats and Ropes if you want. I don't care. It was built up by a man who knew what he was doing. The word is that he has either died or disappeared. I figure he's been murdered because the ranch has been taken over by some gang of outlaws that raid into the Nation and rob travelers in Kansas. They need to be moved out of there."

Quin closed his eyes a moment, thinking the analogy of the gift horse was the correct one. "Hence the badge."

"Hence the badge...and opportunity. It's a job you're very well suited for." Finch smiled expectantly. "If you want to retire and raise horses, here's your chance."

Quin was having trouble finding things to look at besides Finch's exuberant face. "And the legalities? Paperwork? Ownership?"

Finch nodded, rubbing his hands together. "All legal, taken care of by me. The parcel of land is very well surveyed, just in the wrong place."

"Which begs the question. What's in this for you? I know you had to call in some favors to get this badge issued." He knew the Deputy US Marshal's badges were a little harder to come by north of the territory. An Investigator's badge? He'd never heard of that one.

"Money." Finch held his arms wide in an expansive gesture. "You raise cattle or horses and sell to me. Organize your neighbors to sell to me. The army is paying top dollar for good horses, and beef to feed the tribes. I can help build a spur line from the KATY railroad to get close so there's no long drive to market. Also, once a good ranch is established in the area, others will follow."

Quin thought a moment and then nodded. "Now I get it. The railroad contract is the big prize."

"For the most part, yes." Finch grinned. "Lots of money."

"Why not have the army run those boys out of there?" He knew there were several detachments close by in Kansas and Missouri.

"Sorry." Finch was still smiling. "By treaty, The US Army can't go into the territory, where your place technically is located. They cannot interfere. You're a lot more suited for this."

Quin's finger gave the badge a small nudge back toward Finch. "No. I won't need this. I've already quit that job, and decided to quit yours. There must be less contentious jobs somewhere."

The man grinned at him with a dismissive wave. "We'll call it a leave of absence. There's time to think about it. These things take time to wind their way through the hallowed halls of Congress. Take a vacation. Go down and look the area over. If you decide to proceed, send me a telegram and I'll put things in motion. It can't be any simpler than that."

"I'm serious." Quin's reply sounded weak in his own ears. "I'm out of this business. Having a ranch sounds interesting— good, actually. But rooting out a bunch of outlaws is something I don't need. You can hire your own gang to move them out."

"That's not a good option, for many reasons." Finch kept pressing. "Think about it. What will you do, Quin? Wearing the badge is all you know."

"All I know?" Well, that was depressing. Quin stared out the window a moment before continuing. "Maybe I'll find a homestead of my own. Or I could go back to Arkansas and raise weeds and chickens. Find a good woman and raise kids." He got up from the uncomfortable chair and started to leave.

Finch called to him. "Hey, Quin? Don't wait too long."

Quin turned and caught the badge that was tossed at him. After glaring at Finch a moment, he stuffed it in his pocket— right alongside his lucky, worn-out rabbit's foot...which was a conundrum. Lucky for whom? Certainly not the rabbit.

And here he was again, a deputy US Marshal. Sort of.

Chapter Five

There were parts of Kansas City Quin hadn't seen. He'd never come into the stockyards from this high on the bluff, so with time on his hands and a lot of thinking to do, he decided riding a cable car down to the bottoms along the Missouri River was the thing to do.

The ornate Union Station, built at the bottom of the hill, was completed the year before, in 1878. A little farther to the west, he could see builders were making a more sophisticated and elevated line to take passengers down to the bottoms. For now, only a cable car was available that went down what they were calling the ninth street incline, directly to the depot.

To Quin, it looked more like a fancy bucket hooked to a cable and he amazed himself by paying a ticket-seller ten cents for the privilege of riding in it. He wondered why the man sported a real big grin on his face. He found out. His stomach roiled and clenched as that car swayed and rumbled down the bluff.

Riding that car, Quin broke out in his first sweat of the day. If a whole passel of Comanche warriors showed up for breakfast, he wouldn't have been more scared. There was no place he could jump out of that contraption without breaking bones, so he clutched the sides and rode it all the way down.

Once at the bottom, glancing back to the top of the bluff and holding his stomach, he vowed to never make that mistake again—and to have a word or two with that ticket-seller if he had a chance.

On solid ground, Quin's sight-seeing adventure left him gawking around the new Union Depot. It had a clock tower taller than any tree he'd seen, even Arkansas hardwoods and sycamore paled in comparison.

A passerby told him it was over a hundred feet tall. He had tickets to sell too, so Quin didn't believe much the man said. That building stood out like a horse in a herd of donkeys—the donkeys being the train tracks, gambling centers and billiard halls, not to speak of the bath houses and bordellos. It was a place you could get clean, cleaned out, or flat out skinned.

Catering to the cowhands who were usually paid after driving cattle to the stockyards, there were five or six square blocks of any adventure you'd ever want to try, given you had the money, in brightly colored buildings painted gray with train smoke and coal dust.

He should have kept looking and moving, but it was a hot day. Especially in the bottoms where it seemed no breeze circulated. Out to see the sights, it was a bad decision to stop in an establishment with a hand-painted sign advertising gambling and ice-cold drinks. He knew many places stored river ice in buildings insulated with straw. It would be cleaner from ice caves if any were about. But cold is cold.

Any fool knows gambling and whiskey don't mix. He compounded the mistake of entering the parlor, by getting snookered into doing both.

It should have been an innocent and friendly game, if such a thing exists. Several men were present at the card table, but the man running the game had a cockeyed look to him and made a show of having clumsy fingers—trying to convince everyone of his ineptness by dropping a card on occasion with apologies to all. Quin guessed the gambler had a theory. If you think someone is a fumbling card player, you don't watch them for cheating.

Dressed in worn trail clothes, run-down boots, and a short-brimmed hat with a mashed in crown, Quin could see where the man might have thought he was low hanging fruit ripe for the picking.

If the gambler was any good at taking your money, he'd be dealing in the fancy places on top of the hill, or running a bank. The gambler's first mistake was trying a bottom deal. It was a practiced move done with mediocre results and when that card popped up from the bottom of the deck, Quin just stared at him. There were no words spoken after that.

The gambler knew Quin had caught him and then he decided to shoot before he could be named a card cheat. It was close. For a skilled man there is no faster draw than a sleeve gun and the gambler had practiced that too.

The gambler's last mistake was in thinking Quin hadn't already drawn his pistol. Hidden under the table, it was pointed right at the gambler, and that forty-four slug didn't notice the wooden tabletop as it went through. When the gambler raised his hand like pointing at the ceiling, the gesture looked odd enough that Quin knew what was coming. The hand dropped, pointing right at him.

When one of Henry Deringer's finest little pocket pistols peaked out from under the gambler's unbuttoned sleeve, Quin shot him. Fair? Depends on your viewpoint. It was the forty-one-caliber model derringer and would have put a nasty hole in him. If the gambler had asked, Quin would have told him to use the black model, not the shiny silver-plated model that was easy to see. But the man wasn't good at his chosen vocation. Which is why he was dealing from the bottom of the deck in some hole-in-the-wall drinkery.

Normally, the town marshal would run shysters and card artists like that out of town with a stern warning accompanied by a few bruises and a dimple in his hat. Quin guessed the locals hadn't got to this one yet.

Quin didn't want to shoot him. Given a little time, and being close together, he'd have tried for a shoulder wound. But the man was quick with that derringer and gave him no time at all. The gambler was left with a belly wound. If he was lucky, he might die quick. A wound like that was a sure ticket to hell, and sometimes it takes a man days to make the passage. He'd heard laudanum did no good against the pain, but a good many used it to go to sleep and not wake up.

That little fracas left him with a wound high on his shoulder. The bullet notched him as it went by and buried itself in the wall. A man leaning against the wall glanced at the hole in the rough wood next to him and looked a little pale before going to the bar for another drink. Alert to the occasion, the bartender didn't charge.

Tom Speers was the town marshal and walked in while Quin tried to stop the bleeding on his shoulder. Seeing the clumsy job being done, Speers grabbed the neckerchief Quin had folded up and pressed it against the wound. Satisfied it would hold pressure under the shirt, he patted Quin on the other shoulder.

"Why didn't you show them your badge?" Speers' voice was mild.

"Which one?" How did he know of Quin's deputy US Marshal badge?

The man gave him a sour look. "The one that counts."

"You heard about that already?" Quin asked. "The fastest way to an early grave that I know of is to show a deputy marshal's badge to anyone. It's like a sign that says shoot me."

Speers took Quin's good arm and walked them both outside. "This ain't the territory. Quin, you need to leave town. I got a reputation to hold up about no gunfights tolerated. Right now would be a good time to find your horse."

Well now, that didn't set right. "There were witnesses, Tom. He pulled on me first with that fancy little hideout gun, right after a clumsy bottom deal."

"I figured all that." He gazed at the hole-in-the-wall enterprise. "I believe you. But a good number of your witnesses are friends of the man you shot. The owner of this—" he looked with disgust at the people leaving the bar, "—establishment gets a cut of the winnings, so he sure as hell won't be on your side."

"Now Quin just listen a minute." Speers held up a placating hand. "I'll take down everyone's version of the event, which I'm sure will show that you walked in unannounced and murdered an unarmed man playing an honest game, making an instant widow and orphans. Now, he may have orphans, but I'm betting the closest he's come to a wife will be a soiled dove working the upper floor."

Speers continued. "I'll lose that report by the time I get back to the office. It is a windy day. But none of those details matter. You need to be gone before the dust settles. It will make things run smoother around here. I like smooth. Can I get your agreement on that?"

The city marshal handed him the shiny derringer. "You take this, call it the spoils of war. They'll say you stole it anyway, so you might as well have it."

Quin held the little gun. He didn't like them. There was no trigger guard, so when the hammer was cocked the trigger popped out and could catch on anything.

"This is the second time this year I've had to write a report about you." Speers continued, giving Quin a crooked smile. "I can't believe what kind of undesirable reprobate you are. You're a trouble magnet."

Quin checked the makeshift bandage on his shoulder. "You know damned good and well that little fracas down at the stockyards was not my fault."

Speers held up his hands in surrender. "Oh, I know. People are always trying to shoot you—must be your personality. If you don't leave soon, I may try it myself."

That was a good point and Quin thanked him for his foresight. The card-sharp probably did have friends, though he doubted very many, and he didn't want to put the marshal in a bind. And that deal in the stockyards? He'd found some altered brands. It put the supposed owners of that brand in an uncomfortable situation and they acted accordingly.

It was time to see how fat Red had become and see some country.

Chapter Six

After leaving Kansas City, Quin had to admit he cheated. He'd promised not to, but he looked in his journal for the names of the two boys he'd let go home after the shootout. With little to do, he was going to pay a visit to Luke and Josh Samuelson. Maybe he could help out a little.

Like many westerners, he had a good sense of direction so he knew approximately where the homestead was. He didn't miss it far, had to backtrack a little, and finally topped out on a rise with the farm laid out below.

Riding into the barn lot, he was surprised. The fences were up, and a small barn for livestock was built—he'd guess it was put back better than it was before. All in all the place looked neat as a pin.

When he dismounted in front of the house, a small blond woman came out the front door with a curious look. "Good day, sir. May I help you with something?"

"Missus Samuelson, I'm looking for Luke and Josh. I told them I might come by and check on them." Not exactly true, but he was feeling a little off balance. He'd expected a rundown, and dilapidated shoddy. What he saw was a well-put-together operation.

She smiled. "The boys are tending to some chores. Might you be Mister Barrett?"

"I might." He shrugged with a smile. "Depends on whether you're mad or glad."

She laughed at that. "I can be mad or glad in the same shoes, Mister Barrett. With a woman, you just never know what you're going to get."

He'd never heard that expression and vowed to use it again someday. His reply was interrupted by the pounding of horse's hooves and a sudden dust cloud coming around the house.

Two men brought their horses to a standstill. Both were lean and well put together—with concern in their expression. One man asked. "Are you alright, Martha?"

Martha nodded. "Indeed I am, Seth."

Quin looked at the men and then at Martha, wondering what was going on. She didn't look nervous, but two men and a lone woman...?

Giving them a sharp look, he said. "Boys, my name is—"

"We know who you are, Mister Barrett. We saw you when you brought the horses and cattle back to the trail drive. My name is Seth Wooley." He gestured to his partner. "This here is John Purdy."

"I see everything is fixed up real nice around here." Quin said. "Is that you're doing?"

"Oh yes," Martha interjected. "They've been very attentive."

Seth cleared his throat nervously. "Pike paid us off, so we decided to stay and see if we could help get the place fixed up. We felt like we owed that to them." He gave Quin a pointed look. "Don't make this out to be any more than it is."

Martha was colored up some, but stood with her chin up. "These men have been perfect gentlemen and very helpful."

Giving them an amused glance, Quin said. "Look, if everything going on around here is consensual it's none of my business. It appears everything is well taken care of. I just came by to check whether Mister Pike made reparations. In an off-handed way it seems he has. That's my only interest."

Seth snorted. "Pike didn't do anything. That's why we're here."

Quin nodded. That's what he meant by off handed. The trail boss didn't have to let these men go. On the upside, these looked like decent men. "Then that's all I need to know. You folks have a good day, and say hello to the boys for me?"

"We will," Martha said. "Thank you for coming by."

Starting to leave, Quin hesitated by the two riders. "John Purdy? I've heard that name associated with some trouble around Wichita."

Purdy nodded. "I suppose that's me. I can't imagine two of us with the same moniker getting in trouble. Does that bother you in some way?"

"No sir, not at all." Quin said. "Everything I heard was good. The man you helped was a friend."

"Well," Purdy said. "Those days are behind me. I'm trying to quit."

Quin laughed outright, shaking his head, and giving his finger to the hat brim salute again. "Yeah, me too. Y'all have a good day."

He was satisfied everything was under control at the Samuelson homestead. Any considerations or accommodations going on between consenting adults was none of his business. Their arrangement, if what he suspected were true, wouldn't be the first or last. He suspected that would be a first-rate little farm before too long.

Feeling a little light-headed and rubbing his sore shoulder, he pointed Red's nose south, looking for a good place to camp for the night.

Seeing these folks made him think. A nice ranch, well put together and waiting was on his mind. Finch said he had some time to think about it. Since he was headed that way, he decided it would be prudent to check it out on his first opportunity.

~ * ~

A rough trail lay behind him, and each day of traveling made him feel worse. Quin was barely hanging on when he stumbled on the ranch buildings. He figured that gambler's bullet must have been stored in an outhouse. By the time his horse walked into the ranch yard, he had a high fever and could hardly see straight. His shoulder hurt something fierce.

Dave Pinder introduced himself as he stood by Red and offered his hand in friendship and hospitality, with a smile on his face and his other hand on his pistol. Thinking that was two-faced a bit, Quin remembered leaning over to shake his hand. He awoke looking up into the face of an angel holding a wet cloth on his forehead.

He tried twice before his voice worked. "What happened?"

Her smirk wasn't too favorable and her voice was noncommittal. "You fell off your horse."

"That's a first. I'll admit to being bucked off a few times, but I never fell off anything." He centered his gaze on her eyes or tried to. There were two of her, and both looked good. Her hair was dark as a raven's wing, loosely tied in the back with a red ribbon, framing a dusky face set off by dark blue eyes. If he'd ever seen a more beautiful woman, that memory scuttled away into oblivion.

His smile probably didn't work as well as intended. "Did you catch me when I fell?"

She spoke to someone he couldn't see, her sarcasm softened by the twinkle in her eyes. "I think he's getting better."

As she stood to leave, he grabbed her wrist. "What's your name, ma'am?"

Her gaze searched his face a moment before she answered. From her expression he wasn't sure she thought he was worth the effort.

"I am Consuela Pinder. You are on my father's ranch."

As he watched, her eyes deepened in color and her cheeks took on a rosy glow. Kings and conquistadors would fight over this woman in far off lands. He'd read of such and never believed it before. Her arm was warm to the touch and dispelled any idea of her being a dream. He didn't want to let go.

"My name's Quinlan Barrett," he said softly. "Pleased to meet you, ma'am."

Her voice was noncommittal, showing little interest. "Quinlan? What an odd name."

"Call me Quin."

She twisted her wrist in a nifty move to disengage his hand—an experienced maneuver to ward off unwanted attention and done with a smile. "Most folks call me Connie."

"Yes, ma'am." He couldn't keep his gaze off her. "I'll remember that."

"You shouldn't be looking at me like this." Her gaze was finally showing some interest. "If my father notices you'll get bounced out of here.

He sighed, gaze never leaving her blue eyes. "Can't help it."

She stood, shaking her head. "Go back to sleep, cowboy. You're starting to babble like a schoolgirl."

The Pinder ladies were kind, asked no questions and offered a place to rest up until he healed. It was a kindness he appreciated. After they mixed a bitter concoction of leaves with his coffee, and put horse liniment on his wound, he was free of the fever and on his feet in a couple of days. He'd seen yarrow and feverfew growing along the trail, maybe they used those in his coffee—something he should have done himself if he hadn't been so addle-brained.

He did remember hearing a catamount screech when they applied that liniment and he had a whole new appreciation for a horse that just shivers at the application.

After he woke clear-headed, he didn't see much of the Pinders. He kept to the bunkhouse, conversing with the ranch hands when needed. They didn't talk much; he was an outsider and seemed to reflect the attitude of Dave Pinder—friendships are given sparingly.

The ranch appeared small and well-kept. One of the hands pointed out to him that a ride of about twenty miles east would find Joplin, Missouri. The hint wasn't subtle. He also told Quin that Indian Territory, or the Cherokee lands, were just a few miles south. Since his stint of Deputy US Marshal, Quin wasn't a stranger to the territory. After his talk with Thaddeus Finch, had no intention of going any deeper into that land than the mis-placed spread taken over by outlaws.

Since this ranch was in Kansas, the ranch hand was giving Quin a lot of directions to be somewhere else when he got the opportunity. Not knowing if it was personal or instructions passed on from the boss, Quin thanked him for the geography lesson and assured him he'd be on his way soon.

They were a clannish bunch on the Pinder ranch, but that was normal. The ranch hands didn't know him, and trust is earned not given, as it should be. On his second day at the ranch, he was up at dawn helping where he could. Since most cowhands weren't interested in anything they couldn't do from the back of a horse, they watched him with a wary eye, not understanding why he volunteered to milk the two Jerseys or gather eggs. There was a pigpen that was well away from the house, wisely positioned downwind. At least, most days. He carried water to the trough, and then fed them ground corn and any soured milk that might be around, with a few old eggs thrown in for flavor. Judging from the refuse, most of the table scraps went in there too. Pigs will eat anything including people if you're not careful and go anywhere to find the opportunity. Fixing the fence around the pigpen was a daily chore and he made it his.

Not stooping to domestic or farmer labor as they called it, didn't stop the hands from pitching their legs under the table with milk to drink and fried eggs to spice up beef, beans, and potatoes. Adding dried peppers and sour dough bread guaranteed no skinny riders were on the place.

~ * ~

The next time Connie spoke to him was during the great chicken incident. Part of the barn was a henhouse consisting of crates cobbled together and filled with straw to make cubbyholes for their nests. The chickens had to be shut in at night, or they'd be coyote and fox bait. Quin carefully carried a small bucket full of eggs when he stopped in front of that red chicken. If he were to happen to drop those eggs, he'd probably be strung up and shot—in no particular order.

Aside from a rooster, or maybe a turkey buzzard, she was the biggest chicken he'd ever seen. Every time he started to sneak his hand under her to check for eggs, she'd peck him.

One of Quin's failings was not resisting a challenge. He set the bucket down and pulled on leather gloves. Two could play that game. His left hand was reaching for the clucker's neck when Connie came up behind him.

"What on earth are you doing?"

He didn't take his gaze from that chicken because it was damned quick and not above a sneak attack. The chicken had an evil eye no matter which way its head turned. It felt natural when his hand dropped to the butt of his pistol.

"Me and this big red chicken are fixing to come to an understanding. I'm thinking fried chicken, or maybe boiled with potatoes and carrots."

Her soft laugh didn't do his confidence any good as she put her hand on his bad shoulder. It hurt, but he didn't let on. He'd already shown her how loud he could screech.

"Is that the way you treat unruly females? Grab them by the neck?" Her voice was soft, but her eyes mocked him.

His gaze finally broke away from that chicken. "Well, that depends on how bad she's pecking me."

That answer scored no points as she reached under the red clucker with a quick move and come out with two nice-sized eggs. The chicken stared at me while giving a few grumbling clucks to Connie.

Handing me the bucket, she said. "Thanks for your help around here. I mean that. Most men won't do this kind of work. Especially the cowhands."

"Well, I'm not that kind of man."

They stared a little past normal, and then she broke away. "I can see that."

He smiled, hoisting the bucket. "And I like to eat."

She snorted, and then laughed. "You and everyone else around here."

The sun highlighted her as she stopped in the doorway. "I'm curious. Do you always wear a gun doing chores, Mister Barrett?"

"It's just a tool, ma'am. You know the old saying...better to have one and not need it than to need one and not have it." He looked back at the chicken. "So, how do you feel about fried chicken?"

"That's an old hen," she said. "You'd have to boil it."

"I'm sure someone could make dumplings."

The way she laughed; she must have thought he was joking.

~ * ~

Quin spent a lot of time resting on the front porch of the bunk house, and it seemed Connie spent a lot of time checking on him. He couldn't say it was distasteful. A couple of times they saddled up to ride around and get the lay of the land. There was nothing to see but rolling hills covered in grass, with a few trees lining the creeks and watersheds. Their cattle seemed to congregate close to water and shade. Most folks thought Kansas was flat, but the eastern part was not. It was low hills and plenty of water, perfect for cattle and horses. Gardens did well. It was good country.

Loafing in his favorite rocker, he was surprised when Dave Pinder came to talk. Quin closed the worn catalog he was looking at, a finger holding his place for future reading. The section showed women's finery and he would admit to dreaming a bit.

Pinder wasn't known for wasting words, so Quin turned to listen. The chair next to him groaned as it took the man's weight.

"I don't like you spending time with Consuela. I want to make that plain as I can. She's not for someone like you."

Well, that was short and to the point, even for Pinder. This was the first inclination of a problem. "I don't send for her. She comes on her own and is old enough to know her mind."

"I understand that." The man sighed. "She's headstrong, and I'm not surprised she's attracted to a common man. You might suspect she's not my natural daughter."

That gave Quin pause. Pinder had used the word my instead of our. He'd seen the man watching Connie go about her day. It made you wonder how far his possession would go.

Pinder gave a pointed look. "She's mixed blood, I'm not sure what tribe. When she was found outside a burning wikiup by my drovers, they brought her to us. We were childless and we welcomed her as our own."

It hadn't occurred to Quin to wonder about Connie's lineage. Anyone who came from Arkansas as he did had their own set of interesting folks hiding behind the woodpile.

"Who burned the tepee?" Quin asked, looking for a reaction.

"You got a smart mouth." Pinder's gaze sharpened before shaking his head. "Not us. I'm not really good at words. What I'm trying to say is we adopted her and she's to be respected. She carries the Pinder name."

Quin wasn't sure that was a name to be cherished. He still didn't know which side of the fence Pinder was on. Warning him off? Telling him to ride careful? He'd noticed some difference in looks, although Connie's coloring looked enough like Maria's to be a blood relation. All of which wasn't any his business, he couldn't care less. He'd learned not to look under rocks, or behind woodpiles unless you were already sure what was there.

Pinder continued in a rough voice. "I'll be gone a few days moving a herd over to the railhead. They've built loading pens over by Mindenmines and have plenty of stock cars there."

"Mindenmines?" Quin hadn't heard of a spur line there. "That's about twenty miles north of here?"

"More like thirty. Pretty close to the Missouri line. Rumor has it they'll be building this way soon. Some big financier in Kansas City has taken an interest. Anyway, we'll load the cattle and then ride the cars on up to the stockyards in KC. That railroad sure cuts down on time. The hands are going with me. Since you've been doing a lot of riding with Connie I'm guessing you're feeling better? Shoulder healed up?"

His change of subject earned him a cautious look. "Yes, sir. I'm in pretty good shape and ready to go. I owe you a lot of work and appreciate your kindness. I can set a horse and do know one end of a cow critter from the other."

"No doubt you do." The man looked Quin over with a critical eye. "You've repped for that big cattleman's association out of the stockyards. You won't remember, but I saw you there last year. Still checking brands and looking for rustlers?"

"Actually it's a livestock association, not just cattle. I even found a herd of pilfered sheep once." He looked over his shoulder toward the men in the bunkhouse. "I'd appreciate it if you don't mention that anywhere. This is cattle country."

"I won't hold it against you, since they weren't yours." Pinder chuckled, shaking his head.

Quin smiled and nodded gratefully. "I'm not working now. When the town marshal invited me to leave KC, I decided to see some country. Maybe find something to do that I don't get shot at so much."

His look was sharp. "Invited to leave?"

He shrugged, still painful with his wounded shoulder. "I caught a man cheating at poker. He called the hand. I had sixes to beat and he didn't fill."

The man pondered a moment. "I don't like talking in circles. Save the fancy talk for the ladies."

That was fair enough. Quin replied. "I was in a little joint down in The Bottoms, across from that new Union Station, celebrating my retirement. I used poor judgment and sat in a poker game. A gambler tried a bottom deal. When I caught him, he tried to shoot me. He had one of those little sleeve guns on a spring and made a good try. I shot him...didn't have much choice. Tom Speers is the city marshal for that area and invited me to leave town. Since he's a friend of mine, I took his advice."

Quin goaded him a little. "That gambler would have made a good farmer. He had the hands for it."

Pinder gave a short laugh and studied me a moment. "Look, I don't blame you for leaving. And your work was a thankless job. I know some of the cattlemen you've called on—they're always mad about something. The people you worked for aren't much better. Most of them aren't above a little iron work to add numbers to their own herd."

He paused for a moment and then finally got around to it. "I've got a favor to ask. I'm taking all the hands that can ride with me. I'll need them to load the cars and be at the stockyards in KC to mind the pens. I'm hoping that selling them this fall will get us a better price. But mixed herds are always a skittish bunch. I'll lose some if I don't take every rider. Even with all the help, we'll be gone a few days."

Pinder gazed toward the house. "I hate to leave Connie, but it can't be avoided. She rides better than most of my hands and wants to go, but I persuaded her to stay with her mother. And you've seen old Roundy. He can't get around much."

The man raked his glance over Quin. "Roundy won't say it, but I know he appreciates the help around here. So do I. There's more to running a ranch than chasing cows." He chuckled a moment. "I know you carried a badge, so you're trustworthy."

Shaking his head, Quin disagreed. "I wouldn't throw too big a blanket over that. I've seen some tarnished badges."

"Not yours, I'd bet." He smiled at that. "Hell, I shouldn't worry, it's settled country around here. But I do worry. Comes with the job, I guess. I know you're wanting to leave, but will you stick around until I get back? I'd take it as a favor."

Quin thought about it a moment. Watching Connie wasn't hard work—mighty good scenery. And the rancher was right to worry. This country wasn't settled like most people thought and it wasn't the Indians you had to worry about.

The good folks of the world were happy doing their jobs and living day to day. Some were nudging the edges of the law—being as good, or bad, as they wanted or thought they could get away with. And then there were the others that were just plain bad from can see to cain't.

"Alright. I owe you, so I'll stick until you get back." Quin gave him a serious look. "I haven't worked through your wife's donuts yet. Might take a while."

Chapter Seven

The day after the Pinder riders headed their herd to market Connie was again keeping Quin company after breakfast. The morning chores were done, even the crickets were bored of scratching the same tune.

"Riders coming." The soft, low tone of Connie's voice was non-committal and unconcerned, passing the time of day.

They were sitting on homemade rocking chairs that wobbled a little, side to side. Not good enough for the main ranch house, but adequate for the bunkhouse. The bunkhouse itself was more refined than most he'd seen, otherwise he doubted if she would be sitting there.

Quin glanced at her above the old Joplin Herald newspaper in his hands. She might as well have been commenting on the weather. He appreciated her company, although it was a mystery why she wanted to spend time visiting with him. She was the boss's daughter, and that was a line he didn't want to cross. Her father had addressed that in no uncertain terms before he left with all the riders. Of course, given proper motivation, in this case an iron-clad invitation, he'd leap across that line—damn the consequences. But for now, that line was wide and deep.

He guessed her to be about twenty-five, almost a spinster in this day and time, and he was five years older. Was she starved for companionship? Had her father run every suitor away leaving her to age like a fine wine? More than likely she was bored with ranch life and he was something new. It was an interesting subject for speculation on a hot day, sipping tea in the shade.

There was no doubt she would garner attention. She had a trim figure and raven-black hair gained from a possible mixed heritage, he was guessing Spanish and Indian. But there was a fly in her particular ointment. Every day he'd been at the ranch, her temper boiled over at some point. Maybe there was

Irish blood thrown in somewhere. It was odd that a woman so beautiful wasn't married. But with that temper, maybe she didn't fit the mold of docile housewife and might have run off a few suiters herself. Or buried them somewhere. He didn't discount either theory.

Still...it was none of his business. But curiosity and boredom gnaws at your mind. Besides, what else did he have to do with his time, waiting for the boss and crew to return? Idle speculation can keep you sharp or lead you down a rabbit hole.

Scanning the article in the newspaper, he tried to find his place in the story written by a man named Donnelly, telling of a knife-fight in one of the bordellos in Joplin. And the article did seem more embellishment than fact. He'd seen a few knife fights and they rarely lasted more than a few seconds. It was a rare day when two opponents were equally matched and held each other at bay.

The reporter must have needed something to fill up space in the paper since that occurrence would likely take place at least a dozen times a day in that wide-open miner's town. More if you counted shootings. But he did make it sound exciting and Quin admired his writing style, although it wasn't what he'd call a Chamber of Commerce article enticing people to visit.

The paper snapped as he pulled it tight to straighten the wrinkles—being careful because it was over a month old and parts were missing. But it was something to pass the time.

Connie's voice broke his concentration. Again. "What the...? Roundy is running toward the house with his rifle."

That brought Quin out of his chair, wincing in pain at the sudden movement. If that old man was running? Roundy was short and skinny with a hat too big for his head. The newspaper he stuffed inside the sweatband didn't help much. His bowed legs wouldn't let him move much faster than a snail—unless headed for the dinner table. A horse rolled on him years before and he guessed the Pinders kept him on as kind of a pension.

Lately, he and Roundy had formed a partnership in trying to reduce the donut population and the old puncher's speed did surprise him on occasion.

"Mother is by herself in the house. She'll be afraid." Her voice was a little less controlled.

Connie was moving off the porch when he grabbed her. If the riders were unfriendly, running out into the open was the worst thing she could do, and he'd never seen any evidence of her mother fearing anything.

Quin spoke softly. "Hang on a minute. We don't know if anything is wrong. Let's just ease up a bit and see what this is about. Besides, Roundy made it to the house and is with your mother now."

He glanced behind them, uneasy with the situation. In a back corner, inside the bunkhouse, four men played poker for matchsticks. It was a quiet game and the men were studiously ignoring everything around them—too much so. The men rode in a few days before. It appeared they were looking to avoid work and get a free meal. They'd arrived right at the end of the Pinder's roundup and there was plenty of work to do if someone were inclined to help. These men seemed more interested in cleaning their fancy gun-rigs and avoiding sweat.

Except for the Kiowa. Quin didn't know him by any other name, and knew he wasn't lazy. The man just needed the right motivation to move. Gold coin usually had the proper result. He'd used the man for tracking a few times looking for rustlers. The first time they met was a few miles south of Kansas City. Quin was sitting his horse looking at a confluence of tracks all crisscrossing at the same spot when the Indian rode up. "Me Kiowa—good tracker. You pay gold."

Seemed logical to Quin. And the man did a good job.

When Kiowa arrived with the other men, they didn't acknowledge each other. He figured Kiowa knew about the shooting in Kansas City, and that Quin wasn't working. So, no source of gold. That was fair.

Pinder was too kind-hearted toward drifting cowpunchers, which was strange for a bad-tempered man. Quin's own presence was evidence of that, although he pitched in where he could. The men playing poker may never have chased a cow, but they could have helped with feeding the chickens and pigs or pumping water to the milk stock. Their clothes were too good for all that and the tied down holsters would have made it awkward. Between jobs? Maybe. It was 1879, and there were plenty of jobs in Kansas for their type, especially west toward Wichita and Dodge City—or farther into New Mexico.

There was no hesitation in the approaching riders. One pulled up in front of the house and the others cantered their horses over to the corral attached to the barn. They all had pistols out and it didn't take much to know what they were after.

Roundy came out of the main house with his rifle and before he could speak, a bullet fired by the man guarding the porch gouged the wood planks at Roundy's feet leaving a big splinter sticking in the old man's boot.

"Hold up there, old timer. You better drop that rifle before you hurt somebody." The man wore a flat-crowned hat, unshaven cheeks, and an ugly expression. His glance shuttled between Roundy and the men at the corral.

The man didn't shoot the old puncher and that told Quin a lot. He was glad Roundy got smart and laid his rifle down on the porch. At least he hadn't started blasting away at the riders. Maria Pinder was inside the house, and any return shooting might hit her. They used milled lumber to build the house and not logs. A forty-four or forty-five caliber bullet would go through several layers of one-inch pine easy, especially with the new powder being used.

He watched all that play out while grabbing Connie by her dress collar and dragging her back toward the door of the bunkhouse.

"They're after Satan." She struggled against him as the men roped her prized stallion and put a halter on him. It was easy to do since the horse was a pet. He probably thought he was getting his daily apple.

Connie stomped on his foot and then turned and hit him on his sore shoulder, tearing herself free of his grip. Trying to get her back was like stuffing a wet cat in a burlap sack and just as painful.

"Dammit, Quin." She screamed in frustration. "Let go of me."

When she whirled to jump off the bunkhouse porch, she stopped with her hand at her throat.

Four men faced them and they hadn't put away their pistols. One was busy holding the lead rope for the docile stallion.

A scruffy looking man with a full beard and low-crowned dirty hat gigged his horse forward. He had a grin that didn't reach his feral-looking eyes.

"Well now, ain't that something." Scruffy's voice was full of forced humor. "We heard there was a thoroughbred racing stud on this place, just waiting to be taken to market. And here's the matching filly to go with him. Lady, you're coming with us. We'll saddle the stallion for you."

Connie rose to her full height, which wasn't much. Her voice was full of anger and determination. "I will not."

The scruffy man grinned at her. "That wasn't a request. You'll do as I say, or we'll leave everyone dead and have you anyway. You might as well make it easy, but we don't mind if you're dirtied up some—just adds to the fun."

Quin stepped out from the shade of the porch. "Reckon not."

The thief cut a glance at him and laughed. "You're outgunned four to one, mister. Now, you take those pistols out and drop them. We're gonna ride out of here with the stallion and take this woman with us whether you're alive, or not. There ain't a damned thing you can do about it."

His men were getting antsy, cutting glances at one another. It seemed obvious this wasn't part of their plan. Quin moved a couple of steps to the side to get Connie more out of the line of fire. The move put a porch post in front of him. Not much of an edge but it was all he had.

The only one pushing this was Scruffy. The others looked unsure—their guns pointed in the general direction of the porch, but not centered.

A marshal of a cow town in central Kansas once told Quin how he dealt with a mob. Make it personal. Pick out the leader, and make him put up or shut up. Most aren't so brave without the men behind them. Cut him out of the herd.

"You need to make up your mind about this," Quin said. "You've started something that will not have a good ending. If you keep on with this I will take you down, and maybe a couple more with me."

He glanced at the other men. "You men look smart enough. Think about it. This does not have to end in a shooting. I'm hoping you'll reconsider."

Cold eyes watched him a moment, before Scruffy spoke. "You'd draw against all of us? Mister, that's suicide."

Quin shrugged. The man did have a point. "I've been shot at before. To be honest, it's not my first choice for how this plays out. You might be stealing this horse on a lark, just for fun. Or maybe you need the money that bad, I don't know. But make no mistake about it. You try to take this girl, and there will be a killing."

Connie's gaze was flitting between Quin and Scruffy. He thought she was going to speak and gave a quick shake of his head.

A chair leg scraped on the floor inside the bunkhouse and the hair on the back of Quin's neck stood up. He couldn't look, and wanted to in the worst way. Were they coming to help? Or, still sitting and watching.

Scruffy must have been a mind reader. He looked through the window at the card players and settled the question. "Forget it. You ain't got any help coming."

All Quin felt was relief. If those ne'er-do-wells came out it would be a complication. He needed to keep the situation simple, one on one.

"Good," Quin said. "I don't expect any help from them. This is just you and me."

Sighing, he tried to relax. Or at least look like he was before he continued. "Look, we're in no hurry here. You've got the advantage. Take a minute and think about it. The last thing in the world we need is a shooting. Your best choice is to take the horse and get out of here."

Connie looked at him and her burning gaze was hard to ignore. If she had a gun, she'd be shooting—and to hell with the consequences. He admired her spirit, but it gave him a cold sweat at the same time. She needed to keep her temper in check.

He tried to get through to the men one last time. "You might get away with stealing the horse and get good money for him. Then you can take that money and disappear down in the Cherokee Strip until the chase dies down, head for Texas or Old Mexico. I figure that's your plan and you just might make it.

"On the other hand," Quin continued. "If you try to touch this girl, you'll have to go through me. Then, on the off chance you're still alive after that dust-up and do take her, her father and ranch hands will hunt you down and gut all of you. You have to know that."

"You are trading me a horse for the girl?" The thief gave an uneasy laugh. "Hell, I already have the horse. If we're caught, they'll hang us for horse stealing anyway. Might as well have the whole package and a few comforts along the way. What's that saying? In for a penny...?"

Quin sighed. "Alright, have it your way. I've already picked a button on your shirt. I figure at this distance, I can't miss."

This was dragging out way too long, but the man looked unsure. Quin tried again. "Don't be stupid. You'll have to shoot across your horse, and he's skittish already. That pistol of yours weighs about three and a half pounds and you've been holding it a while. Think you can get a straight shot at me? First try?"

Quin shook his head. "Your first shot will miss. By the time you thumb that hammer back again, you'll be dead." His glance covered them all. "And your boys will have to shoot across his body to get to me. I'm on steady ground. Even if y'all put lead in me, I'll kill some of you. I'm settled in that. You boys want to chance it?"

Scruffy snorted. "Nobody's that fast."

"I am." Quin replied in a cold, steady voice.

"It's worth the risk." Scruffy's gaze traveled over Connie in a way that made her gasp and step back. "That's a fine-looking woman, and I think you're bluffing."

The men behind him backed their horses and turned to go. One of them commented, "C'mon Jonas. This ain't right and you know it. We didn't sign up for this."

Jonas sighed, shrugged, and then gathered the reins on his horse. His advantage was backing away and leaving. He stopped for a moment, staring at Quin. "Who are you?"

Quin smiled, still watchful. "Nobody you'd know. The only reason I'm here is because the owner told me if I'd hold down one of those chairs on the porch, he'd feed me once a day—my horse too. I've tried to leave a couple of times, but I can't convince my horse to go."

"Funny. You're just a drifter looking for a handout, like that riffraff in the bunkhouse? I'm not buying that. You're too damned calm about all this, like you're not worried at all." The man shook his head. "Everyone's got a name. You got sand, mister. I'll give you that. Since my idiot partner already gave you my name, I'll finish it. I'm Jonas Macrae. Most people have heard of me. I'd like to know who you are."

Quin knew the name. Macrae was on most lawmen's wanted list of being rumored, but not proven, to be a rustler and thief. A bad man in the oldest sense. An old wildness was building in Quin as he watched Macrae's gun. If it moved toward him or Connie, he was going to try.

"The name is Quinlan Barrett."

The outlaw stared at Quin a moment and then dropped his reins around his saddle horn and rubbed his face, canting his hat back. "I can't believe I'm doing this. Never heard of you at all. You look like a fighter. I know most everyone in the business."

"That's because I'm not in your business." Quin shrugged. "There's no reason you should know me. I'm just a man likes to sit on the porch and read a good book, maybe talk to a pretty girl occasionally."

It was Quin's turn to smile. "You've got something to hang your hat on when this story is told."

"What's that?" Macrae gave him a curious look as he settled his hat and gathered the reins again.

Quin replied. "You said I'm a nobody. You can still say *nobody* has ever backed you up."

"You're trying to be funny again. I don't get it." Giving them a puzzled glance, Macrae shook his head. Still pointing pistols at them, the riders backed their horses away. Once past the house and out of pistol range they turned and rode from the ranch with a whoop and a couple of shots fired in the air, leading the stallion.

Chapter Eight

Quin shook his head slowly, and let out a relieved breath. Those men must have been three days drunk when they decided on their little excursion. But they'd pulled it off with little or no trouble.

Connie interrupted his sigh when she turned and shoved him. "You could have stopped them. I don't know why, but they were afraid of you and you let them get away with my horse."

She wiped tears from her eyes with the back of her hand as he caught his balance. When she tried to shove him again, he caught her arms. "Will you stop? And no ma'am. Those men were not afraid of me. Not one bit."

"But...?" She was trying to talk to fast and nothing came out.

He had to let her go or someone needed to play a tune. Personally he could go either way, but they had more serious matters to attend to. "Look. I was trying to avoid a lot of people getting dead. I gave those men choices. They weighed the cost and made the right decision. They weren't out to kill anybody, just steal a horse and make some money. I'm glad it went the way it did. No one needed to get killed today."

Her violent head shake tumbled hair down over her face. "You could have told them to leave the horse. They would have done it."

"They weren't going to leave empty handed." Shrugging, he turned away. "Like Macrae said, it was a trade. Everyone gets something in a trade."

Her face was ruddy in anger, jaw clenched tight enough to turn her cheeks white. "A trade? I lost the finest horse in this part of the country. What did you get?"

His gaze took her in, head to toe. "You, although I'm beginning to doubt my sanity."

She stomped so hard it moved one of the rockers. "We could have fought it out."

"We? You hiding a pistol somewhere I can't see? One man had the drop on Roundy, the others were pointing pistols at us already—and those deadbeats inside are worse than useless, so by now, we'd be dead or shot-up bad."

He pointed a finger at her. "And provided you survived, you and your mother would be on your way to a hard life. After those men finished using you, they'd kill you or sell you to a whorehouse. It's happened before. Is that what you want? You'd do that to your mother?"

Lowering his arm, he shrugged. "And if they didn't kill me, your father would put the boots to me for not protecting you. Can you get that through your little pea-brain for one minute?"

For once, she was speechless as he walked toward the main house. Maria Pinder came out of the door as Quin stooped and picked up the discarded rifle and handed it to Roundy.

"Are you doing okay, Roundy?" Quin looked the man over to make sure he wasn't hurt.

"Well... Quin, I...." The old man's voice quavered.

Quin's hand went to the oldster's shoulder. "You handled that just right. Nobody got hurt."

Roundy looked embarrassed. Maybe he felt shamed in front of the women. "I should have done something."

"No. You shouldn't have." Quin met his gaze. "There's a time for fighting, and this wasn't it. We had no advantage. Think about what would have happened to the women if we'd started shooting. Five of them and two of us? We might have lost, Roundy. Probably would have. And if the gunfire didn't kill the women, their fate would have been far worse. You know that."

Roundy stood a little taller. Quin didn't point out that Roundy could have dropped his man from inside the house when they rode up and then they would have had the rustlers in a crossfire. That would have changed things considerable and given them a fighting chance, possibly running them off empty-handed. But that didn't happen. Once Roundy stepped out on the ranch house veranda, the die was cast and they had no chance at all.

"Besides," Quin squeezed Roundy's shoulder again. "When we meet those boys again it'll be on our terms, not theirs.

Once you steal something and start running, you can never stop."

Footfalls and the jingle of fancy spurs announced the arrival of the bunkhouse lay-abouts. Quin didn't spare them a glance. "Roundy you keep your rifle on those deadbeats coming up from the bunkhouse. I don't like coincidences."

He turned to Connie's mother. "Missus Pinder? Are you doing alright?"

From the way her dress hung down on one side he guessed she had a pistol stuck in her pocket. Had those men busted in her door they'd have got a big surprise.

Missus Pinder nodded. "Please call me Maria. I'm considerably better now that those men are gone. Thank you for dealing with this, Mister Barrett. And I agree with your assessment. Except for that one man, the rest of those thieves did not seem disposed to shoot unless we forced them."

She paused, looking in the direction the riders went. "Although, I suspect they'll hang for it anyway. I just wish my Dave was here."

Quin shrugged, rubbing his sore shoulder. "It's not your husband's fault. Those cattle wouldn't deliver themselves. You know that. He'll be back soon enough. Nobody died, and all we lost was a horse. That's just about the best ending to this we could have."

Maria's gaze hardened as she looked at something behind him. "Those men weren't any help."

The card players were sauntering toward them. Their leader was a man called Chico—at least, that's the name others called him. Seemed to Quin that every county in the southwest had a Chico and he was always a bad man. This one was about as Mexican as an Irish track layer. Quin hadn't taken the time to learn names for the other two. Mostly, he ignored them all week.

Kiowa was the fourth man, and he was standing in front of the bunkhouse, with a rifle across the saddle of his horse. It must have already been saddled. Was he thinking ahead or getting ready to leave before this happened? His gun was pointed more toward the three card players, but Quin wouldn't want to stake his life on who's side the man was on.

Taking a chance, he nodded to him and then pointed to the trail the horse thieves took. Kiowa hesitated a moment and then leaped on his horse and rode around the barn. Knowing he usually liked his money up front; it was a tossup whether he would trail the thieves or call it a day and disappear into the Nation. Quin turned his attention back to the other men.

"You boys volunteering to go after those horse thieves?"

Chico smiled and spread his arms wide. "Perhaps? For a price we might be willing to find these men?"

Quin didn't like the idea, but it wasn't his call. Before he could speak, Maria stepped forward.

"You had your chance to help and did not," she said. "Now you saddle up and leave. My husband has a soft spot for drifters and bums. I do not."

"Now, you listen here...."

Quin took a step toward him. Most western men were respectful of women. He seemed to be running into a lot of the other breed lately.

"You be real careful with what comes out of your mouth next, Chico. This family put you up for a week and fed you. You've done nothing in return but lay about playing poker and sleeping. You could have helped stop those horse thieves and chose to sit and watch. Now, you'll ride."

Roundy broke in with a rough voice. "Quin, those thieves knew about that horse and went straight to him. How'd they know? And they must have known our crew was gone on roundup or they wouldn't have waltzed in here like they did."

The double-click of a cocking pistol behind him was a surprise, along with the sound of two rifles loading shells. He grinned at Chico, knowing the trio behind him were ready.

"Reckon y'all better leave. Right now would be a good time to start. We've been trying to avoid trouble this morning, but you could be the exception. And boys. You just take what you came with...nothing extra."

A few minutes later, they stood on the veranda of the house watching the men ride away with a flurry of curses and dirt clods. Roundy took off his hat and scratched his balding pate.

"Now, I don't suppose them riding off in the same direction as those thieves was an accident?"

Quin glanced at him. "Maybe, maybe not. Joplin's to the east—just a whole lot of nothing west of here until you hit Wichita. And the horse thieves? I don't think they'll go far. I'm thinking they need money and have a fondness for what it will buy them."

The old man gave him a sidelong glance. "Nine of them now, if they're in this together."

He watched Connie and her mother move back inside. "Might be eight. The jury is still out on the Kiowa."

"Now." Quin hesitated a moment and then continued. "I'm wondering where they'd go to sell a racehorse?"

Roundy didn't hesitate. "Racetrack over at Galena, little bit southwest of Joplin. They have a race about once a week. Most times on a Sunday."

"Let's think about that a moment," Quin said. "Few people around the racetrack would have the money to buy a horse like that. Most times, the owners aren't there. I'm thinking the serious money is in Joplin, or maybe Carthage. That horse won't sell cheap."

Soft steps marched up next to him and he turned to see Connie, dressed for the trail. A red ribbon kept her hair swept up behind her, and a flat-crowned hat covered most of it. Her father mentioned she could ride, and she wore a working hat that had seen equal amounts of sweat and dust. The times they'd ridden together she didn't wear a hat.

"Going for a ride?" Quin asked mildly.

Her gaze was all cold blue eyes and her mouth made a grim line across her face. "Those bastards stole my horse. I'm going after them, even if you won't."

Maria came out behind her daughter, wringing her hands and shaking her head. Her voice was exasperated. "I can't stop her. She's bound and determined."

"You can't go." Quin held up his hand as Connie started to argue. "I promised your father I'd look after all of you until he gets back. That includes your mother. If you leave, I go with you. Don't pretend you don't know that. Do you want to leave your mother here alone? What if those men take a notion and circle back? Our best bet is to stay put until your father returns with the men."

Connie shook her head. "Roundy can stay with her."

The old man scuffed the wooden floor with his boot. "I ain't much help, miss. Proved that already."

"We can't sit around and do nothing." Connie's voice weakened as she glanced at her mother and then settled her gaze on Quin. He knew what she was thinking. She thought him a coward for not stopping the horse thieves.

He glanced at Maria. "How long until Mister Pinder and the hands are back?"

"It will be a few days and I know you can't wait that long." Maria paused a moment. "Might I offer a suggestion?"

Quin grinned at her. "Somebody better. We're talking in circles, and your daughter is about to shoot me."

She laughed and nodded. "There's a new settlement called Hard Times between here and Joplin. Well, part of it's new. The people in the old town might wish the new businesses would go away. They're mostly gamblers and bawdy house owners."

"Mother?" Connie's voice was shocked although her expression was amused.

"Oh, come on Connie. I wasn't born under a rock, and neither were you. You can't keep something from existing by not thinking or talking about it. Anyway," she turned back to Quin. "I have a friend that lives outside of the old part of town, Irma Baker. She lost her husband and then her son was killed last year. I'd like to visit. Roundy can stay and look after the place while we're gone and then let Dave know what's going on when he shows up. After I'm delivered to my friend, I'll be safe enough there, you two can try to find the horse. I don't hold much hope in that, but I know you must try. Is that something we can all live with?"

Quin tipped his hat to her. "That's why you're the boss, ma'am. Do you have enough money to buy the horse back?"

"What?" Connie whirled on him. "I thought you were a man. Somebody steals my horse while you stand and watch, and then you want to buy him back? Of all the foppish, limp-wristed—"

He raised his hand and she stopped talking with a startled look. Quin was surprised at that. Surely, she didn't think he could hit her. Not in this lifetime. Had somebody...?

"Cool down and think about this. Let's say we find the horse. When you run up against these folks in a crowd, or bring a sheriff once you find them, how can you prove the horse is yours? Last I saw, there was no brand on him. Well, I sure wouldn't be surprised if there isn't a brand on him now.

And not yours. Or are you going to grab your rifle and just start blasting away?"

Connie stared long and hard at him a moment. Finally, her shoulders slumped. "We didn't brand Satan because I didn't want to hurt him. He's so beautiful. I raised him from a colt. And a brand is just a big burn scar."

Quin nodded, shrugged, speaking softly. "No doubt. And he's a real pretty horse—makes a fine show strutting around. I'm sure there's not a mark on him. I'd bet he's limp from hoof to mane, scared to death of a mare with a little spirit, but who's gonna tell. I mean, with him being so pretty and all."

Her ruddy complexion seemed to pale as she reached out toward him. "I'm sorry. I didn't think...."

"No, ma'am. You did not." Quin said.

Her boots left little dust explosions as she stomped off toward the barn. She was mad, but it was sure hard to ignore her walk.

Maria sighed and then continued in a soft voice. "Like I said. Spoiled and headstrong. Dave and I are to blame for that. But she's a good person. And she likes you. Know that? She just doesn't have much experience in letting you know."

His next words came unbidden. "I'm surprised she isn't married."

Chuckling, she said. "No one has ever come around that piqued her interest."

She gave him a side-long look. "Until now. And come to think of it, why aren't *you* married? A double harness isn't all that bad."

"Never been caught...." His voice trailed off, the word *yet* was obvious, but unspoken. "It might depend on what you're harnessed with. Looks to me like she hates the ground I walk on."

Maria's laugh was infectious. "If you think that, you don't know much about women."

Roundy smothered a laugh.

"You got something to say?" Quin tried to look mean, but it wasn't in him.

When Roundy didn't answer, other than grin, Quin answered her. "You're right about that. At least, not a good woman like her. Although I'm not sure anyone can know her. She seems a might flighty."

Maria patted him on the shoulder. "You haven't noticed her hanging around you, dressing nice—trying to stop acting like a tom-boy? Most of us hadn't seen her in a dress for a long time, except for an occasional Sunday meeting."

That made him chuckle. "Oh, I noticed. I'm not blind, and your daughter is a beautiful woman. I'm a little skittish about that...not sure how you...well, Mister Pinder warned me off. And we've just met."

"It's been over two weeks. My husband knew how the wind was blowing before he left. He may not like it, I'm sure he doesn't, but you're still here. That should tell you something. Don't let him run a bluff on you." She paused a moment, her expression troubled. "On the other hand, be careful around him. He has unstable moments that worry me. It seems that lately there are more of them."

Quin nodded. "Thanks for the warning, ma'am. I'll tread lightly."

Chapter Nine

"**N**ow." After their discussion that turned serious, Quin was startled when Maria clapped her hands together and turned all business. "Roundy, please bring the buckboard around. If we hurry, we can make it to Edna's place before dark."

Thinking he'd better hurry or get trampled in the rush, he moved to the barn. Connie already had the horses saddled when he got there. The Texas saddles were heavy, but didn't stand a chance against her anger. He could hear her mumbling as he walked in. Dust explosions danced on sunlight streaming through the hayloft door, giving the interior a golden glow set off by dark shadows. A slight movement brought his gaze to a big yellow cat licking its paw—unimpressed with the people in its barn.

He paused while Connie pounded her fist on the saddle of her horse. She'd been attentive to him all week and though he acted unaffected—it was a lie. Anytime he thought of her showing interest in him, her sanity was in doubt.

Quin spoke softly. "Is that some new way to settle down a horse, or just an unruly saddle?"

She flinched and then glanced at him. Tears coursed down her cheeks and blended with her freckles. Her voice was soft and rough from the dust she'd stirred up.

"Please, Quin. I regret speaking the way I did. I don't know what's got into me lately. Seems half the time I don't know who I am—other times I don't want to know."

He leaned against the same saddle she was beating, close enough that her faint scent overrode the horse smells wafting through the barn. Gently, he wiped her tears away. She gave him a startled glance, it was their first touch, and then she relaxed with a sigh and leaned into his palm a moment.

When they confronted the horse thieves, he'd known an unnatural fear. Not for himself. It was the fear that someone he cared for might be hurt—a fear steeped in helplessness. He'd read somewhere that if you love someone then you're a hostage to worry. Now, he understood.

His words were not eloquent, though he wished them to be. "It's alright, ma'am. No harm done."

Her gaze was on the strap and buckle of a saddlebag she fiddled with. "Stop calling me ma'am. It makes me feel old."

"Can't."

That got her attention and she gave him a curious look. "And why not?"

He glanced at her as he led his horse outside. "You haven't kissed me yet."

The expected explosion didn't come. When he looked back, she was smiling. That scared him, too. It was a poor way to start a day...being afraid. Twice.

Roundy was outside with the buckboard. When he got Missus Pinder situated, he handed Connie a Winchester for her saddle boot. His eyebrows raised when he looked at Quin's shotgun hanging by a loop.

"Don't you want a rifle?" The old man groused. "We got a Henry inside that's a spare."

"No, thanks." Quin took off his hat, wiping his brow before reseating it. "Heard a story once, about a stage driver being held up by a would-be bandit. Well, the driver went to shoot the miscreant and his Henry rifle jammed. Way he tells it, the only reason he survived the day was because the outlaw had a Henry and it jammed, too."

His glance caught the women rolling their eyes. "It may not be true, but this old coach gun will work for me. I'm not looking for a long-range war. And it's good for most varmints, two-legged or four."

Quin gave Roundy a serious look. "Speaking of varmints, you watch out for that red hen. She's got an evil look to her."

There was no road leading to Hard Times, at least not from the ranch, which made Maria Pinder's choice of taking a wagon for the trip dubious, at best. She seemed spry enough to ride a horse, and he chafed at the slow going.

Connie seemed content to ride alongside her mother, and he let them guide the way. They seemed to know where they were going. He tried to ride far enough back to stay out of the dust, hoping for a breeze strong enough to clear the air. He rode to the side on occasion to look for sign of the deadbeats they'd run off from the ranch.

Finding her pet stallion would not be easy. Proving it was hers would be impossible. That left few alternatives. If he found the horse, they'd have to take it back by force. His sense of it was Jonas Macrae wouldn't give up without a fight. He seemed a prideful man and dressed himself well enough that turning to thievery seemed unlikely if lack of money was an issue. Some people never understood the concept of ownership. If Macrae had some other plan working, Quin couldn't figure it out. Mysteries are fun to read about, but a pain in the backside in real life.

They stopped for a nooning in the shade of a sycamore tree. In this part of the country the trees were prevalent, especially near water. A muddy stream made lazy passage nearby, but he didn't like the looks of it. He soon had water boiling for coffee and the ladies broke out bread and cheese from a wicker basket.

Maria was taking her cup to the stream when he stopped her. "Ma'am let's boil this water and add some coffee to it. We'll drink that until something better comes along. That stream water doesn't look good to me. You might notice that the horses won't go near it."

She cast a baleful eye at the stream, nodded her head and returned to the wagon.

"So, what is your plan, Mister Barrett?" Connie's voice was mocking as she sat on the wagon gate. "How shall we get my horse back?"

"When I have a plan, you'll be the first to know."

She gave him a mocking glance. "I thought you were a detective for some cattleman's association. This would seem to be an easy job for a man of your experience."

His gaze met hers over the top of his tin cup. Two weeks wasn't a long time to get to know someone. He couldn't separate sarcasm from accusation, nor tell if she was digging her spurs in his side just to get a rise out of him.

"It was a livestock association, not just cattle. We gave equal importance to sheep, goats, or even camels. A man had a couple of camels disappear...said they were leftovers from the army and their campaign into old Mexico. I never did find them." He glanced at her from under his hat brim. "You may have an over-embellished view of my last job. But to go along with that, if someone complained of losing cattle, or that their neighbor was selling more cattle than they could possibly raise, the association would send me out to look around. If I found evidence of cows dropping a half-dozen calves at a time, I'd report it to the local authorities. That's all."

Connie shared an amused glance with her mother. "And those you investigated never objected? You never had to use those pistols you wear all the time—especially the one you're tapping with your fingers right now? I've noticed it's never far from your hand. Gonna shoot me? You're going to have to replace the grips soon. That walnut is worn smooth from use."

When he gave her a sour expression and didn't rise to the bait, she continued. "My father pointed out a few things, just to warn me away from you. He mentioned those flashy gun-rigs those deadbeats in the bunkhouse polished all the time and didn't show much use. That lack of wear and tear was the opposite of yours that's functional and damned near worn out. You also came to us wounded. I assume that wasn't because you dropped your gun and it went off."

"Connie." Maria's voice was soft in admonition. He had a sneaking suspicion she was laughing.

"No, Mother. He's not going to get away with this...this...act of a mild-mannered drifter just out to see the world. He's more than that. Even wounded, his gun was never far from his hand. I'm not blind, and I want to know who, or what he is...not what he claims to be."

Quin sighed and stepped over to Red, rummaging around in one of the saddlebags. Pulling out a small book, he leafed through the pages a moment and then showed it to her.

"Have you read this? It's one of Frank Starr's pocket novels. I got it for a nickel from a whiskey drummer before I left Kansas City. This one is numbered one hundred thirty-nine and is all about Kit Carson, called The Fighting Trapper. I figure there must be at least a hundred thirty-eight books before this one and they're all about gun slicks and fast draw artists, mountain men and town-tamers—some real, famous men. Each one a hero. Why, it's unbelievable what some of those characters do, or the predicaments they shoot themselves out of. It makes great reading and fine adventure. Maybe you can find yourself a hero in one of those stories."

His gaze leveled on her. "But it won't be me. I'm just a man. No more, no less. And I'm certainly no hero."

"You...you...." She stomped her boot in the dust and stalked over to her horse. The poor critter was startled when she kneed its belly, driving out its wind so she could tighten the cinch. He vowed to watch out for that knee in the future.

Connie's mother had put things away during our show and climbed up in the wagon seat. Her shoulders shook. She'd been doing a lot of that and he couldn't tell if she was laughing or crying. She slapped the reins over the horse's backs and pulled away. Connie rode next to the wagon, stiff-backed and tight lipped.

Quin didn't like being confused, and was unsure of his part in this play. Maybe that was by design. By the time he'd kicked dirt over the little fire he'd built, dumped the coffee, and cleaned the pot in the murky stream they were out of sight.

That brought him up short. He needed to get a handle on his own frustration before it killed him. He'd just cleaned a coffee pot in a stream he wouldn't drink water from. People die of cholera, or any number of things from bad water. It wasn't pretty. Or died from bad decisions. He'd add that one to the list.

Chapter Ten

It didn't take long to catch up to the ladies. They'd stopped just around a small hill, about a half mile away. They were using a well-traveled trail by now, and Kiowa sat his horse in the middle of it unperturbed by the business ends of two rifles pointed at him. Quin was pleased to see him, thinking the man was long gone.

Kiowa nodded when he saw him. "Quin. You come."

Stopping beside Connie, he gently pushed the barrel of her rifle down. Gently, because her finger was on the trigger, and if he knew anything about her, that finger was taking up slack already.

"He's on our side, ladies." As he rode past, Connie started to follow. "Stay with your mother. If it's something you need to see, I'll come get you."

He didn't get a promise from her, but should have. As they moved toward a cottonwood grove, he could see a tendril of smoke drifting on the breeze from a small campfire. The jingling of harness, hoofbeats, and creaking of the wagon followed behind him. Seemed that taking orders wasn't in the Pinder women's lineage.

It was an odd feeling. One he didn't like. They'd been taking a noon meal less than a half-mile from death. Kiowa had been riding around the hills undetected. Quin couldn't figure out where his head and senses were until he looked around at Connie. Her expressionless gaze looked back at him, except for one eyebrow reaching impossible heights. Watching her, he knew distraction had a name.

Kiowa didn't need to say anything. The story was already laid out. The why and how, maybe the who, just needed to be filled in.

Four bodies lay around the dying fire wrapped in blankets, whiskey bottles scattered close to hand—none had a drop left which was curious. You can pour a bottle empty, each and every one. It would be odd to drink them all empty. There was a blackened pot sitting to one side of the coals. If they were all drunk, who was drinking coffee?

The first impression to someone coming onto this camp might have been that the men were sleeping off a night of revelry, but Quin knew these men left the ranch a couple of hours ahead of his own party. In a sense, they were asleep. Three of the men had ear-to-ear smiles somewhat below their chins. A bullet hole in the chest took care of the fourth man. His blanket lay to the side. Quin's guess was the man heard something—or wasn't as sound asleep as the murderer thought, and died the hard way.

Nothing made sense. They were dead actors frozen in a scene of a play. If they were drunk, they might be sleeping in the middle of the day. But they weren't. Blankets were thrown on top of them, but no ground sheets under them. Saddles were used as head rests, but their necks and heads were at odd angles. Their throats were cut, but no blood where they lay. There were obvious heel marks on the ground from where they'd been dragged away from the fire. Again, why? It seemed a large amount of work for little chance of duplicity.

"These are the men who helped steal the stallion." Quin stated the obvious as he looked at Kiowa.

The man shrugged, moving away.

Quin's voice stopped Kiowa a moment. "I wouldn't drink any of that coffee, and be sure to stomp that pot flat before you throw it away. We wouldn't want anyone else to use it."

The stream they'd just camped beside might make you sick enough to die but it would not be today and not a quick death. If this was a celebration for a successful horse-stealing, his guess was the coffee came first to their party and had something added to make the men sleepy. Someone staged the rest—for what purpose, he wasn't sure. Of course, anyone else coming up on this wouldn't know what Quin did about the men. Did the killer think a passerby would assume they were drunk and asleep and not disturb them?

And why not let them die of poison? Maybe time was a constraint? A sick man can pull a trigger, so someone stayed and assumed friendship to the last drop. And then, made sure. That was a coldness hard to contemplate. This was done by someone who liked what they were doing.

Riding a slow circle around the camp didn't supply much information. The dead men's mounts were hobbled in the grass next to that muddy creek. Judging by the tracks, their horses wouldn't drink it either. Conspicuous by their absence were Jonas Macrae and a certain pet stallion called Satan.

Kiowa didn't tell him anything he didn't already know. He pointed east. "One rider, leading the horse."

Dismounting, Quin walked among the bodies. When he moved the blankets, he found their pockets turned out. Saddles and tack were stacked next to their bedrolls. Their saddlebags and possible bags lay empty on the ground. He kicked over that coffee pot.

Turning, he spoke to Kiowa. He had a strong feeling the man had already checked the bodies. "These were thieves and not worth much consideration. I don't care about their guns and horses. But if there are papers showing who they were, I need to turn them over to a marshal so he can notify next of kin. Their relatives should know."

Kiowa stared at him a moment. Quin had just given the man a small fortune and he knew it. An average horse sold for around a hundred dollars, the rifles about fifty dollars, and the pistols sold new for seventeen dollars. That was a good haul. Kiowa's face was impassive when he shrugged. "No papers."

At Quin's surprised look, Kiowa hastened to reply. "Pockets already pulled out. Saddlebag's empty. No papers. No money."

Macrae was a known thief. He'd take their money or anything else of value. But packing around extra rifles and pistols would be conspicuous. People would ask questions. The same for extra horses. If a marshal identified the bodies, that in turn might lead back to the killer as people the murderer was known to travel with. It was reasonable to think Macrae would bury any papers or letters.

According to the ladies the nearest town was east of them, a small spring-up called Hard Times. It was another reasonable assumption Macrae would head there before moving on to the bigger town of Joplin, or maybe the county seat of Carthage. He probably had money to spend and a horse to sell.

Quin didn't know what drove Macrae, what his hunger was, but he'd bet the man would feed it soon. He'd read of certain types of people who killed for pleasure and then that pleasure became a need, much like opium or laudanum. That kind of hunger must be fed and often.

When he started to dig in his pocket for a gold piece to pay off Kiowa, the man rode close and shook his head. "No money. Job not done. I stay."

"What about—"

Kiowa nodded toward the horses. A couple of men had materialized. Wearing range clothes and slouched on good horses, their braided hair fell from beneath floppy hats.

Quin figured everything but the bodies would disappear into the Nation a few miles south. The obvious question went through his mind as his gaze snapped back to Kiowa.

The man's smile was mocking. "We no kill these men." He shrugged. "Could have. Easy."

He was right. And if Kiowa and his friends wanted Quin and the women dead, they were easy targets too. Those men helping Kiowa were like ghosts.

Watching the men work at gathering all the supplies and anything else worth something, he sighed. He was beginning to think retirement somewhere peaceful was a good idea. If he ever had a knack for this sort of thing, he was losing it. Some of the heroes in the books he read stumbled fecklessly through life altering situations while those around them saved the day. He did not want to be that man.

"Alright." Quin nodded to Kiowa. "Be sure to tell them to eat or drink nothing from the camp. I'm thinking these men were poisoned, or at least made drowsy, before they were killed."

Kiowa walked his horse over to the two men, talked a moment and then rode east.

Connie spoke up from behind Quin. He was amazed she'd been quiet this long. "Aren't you going to bury those men?"

"Nope." Quin settled his hat firmly on his head, taking a last gaze at the campsite.

"You can't just—"

He interrupted. "You mean I should give a Christian burial to men who would gladly murder or rape you and your mother? The same men you wanted me to kill in the first place just to save a dumb animal? Those men?"

Her head shook slowly as color rose to her cheeks. "We are Christian by what we do, how we act."

"You're correct on that point. Apparently I'm not that good a Christian. With all due respect." He tipped his hat. "Ma'am."

After giving him a scathing look, she turned her horse and rode away.

"That's what I thought." It was a weak rejoinder and acknowledged by the look on her mother's face as she turned the wagon around. If Maria was keeping score in whatever game was being played, he wasn't doing well.

The small cavalcade returned to its journey. One thing was certain. Connie's supposed infatuation with Quin was at an end. He wasn't proving up to her expectations. Maybe that was a good thing? What did he have to offer? And if it was a good thing that she wasn't interested and he was settled in that notion, why didn't he feel better?

He turned in the saddle and looked at the campsite one last time. It was another mystery. Why the charade done in haste? Who would care? A shadow crossed the ground in front of him. He didn't need to glance up. Buzzards. Nature's cleanup crew. They were patient and would wait for all of them to clear out. Maybe they cared.

Chapter Eleven

The rest of the journey was uneventful. Winding through low hills and gullies, fording an occasional slow-moving and muddy-bottomed stream, the warm afternoon could lull the senses if they didn't have so much on their minds.

Even from miles away, the clear air was marred in the east by the smokestacks of smelters in the Joplin area, burning coal to melt the ore pulled from the shallow mines. Quin knew they'd started as silver mines, but the money was being made from what they called jack—the zinc byproduct of the smelting process. Factories were using zinc for everything from lining buckets to making paint and whitewash last longer.

The downside of the huge array of free enterprise going on was a wide-open town with law and order a mere suggestion, ruining the ground like runaway moles, and turning the water runoff into a dirty brown sludge you could smell long before you saw it. He wouldn't be surprised if a good, clean cask of water wouldn't sell higher than a bottle of whiskey.

A couple of miles west of Hard Times, they pulled into the yard of a ramshackle house an hour before sundown. A slat-thin woman in a shapeless and threadbare dress with the floral print washed out of it watched from an open doorway, shading her eyes with her hand. Moments later, the three women met in a group hug on the porch.

Connie spoke to Quin before the women went inside. Her expression was neutral; a surprise, considering her temperament. In their short acquaintance, he'd never seen her ambivalent about anything.

"We'll stay here tonight," she said. "Please let me know if you find my horse." Abrupt, not waiting for an answer before she turned away without a second look.

The dismissal stung, but was alright in a sense. He didn't have anything much to say to her anyway. Turning his horse, he rode toward Hard Times. All he'd heard of the place was not good. A pop-up town trying to keep pace with the runaway and bawdy reputation of Joplin, Missouri. If Joplin were the whale, Hard Times would be the underbelly—every decision in the town based on whiskey consumption and greed.

A perfect place for a killer and thief.

The town had two streets. The new part was perpendicular to the old, and pointed straight east toward Joplin. Both sides of the new street reminded Quin of The Bottoms in Kansas City. There were gambling halls, bath houses, and rooming houses where you could hot-bunk with your soiled dove of the evening, or sleep alone after you'd been fleeced of every dollar.

Kiowa sat his horse at one end of a short street in the old, original part of town, watching the blades of a windmill turning slow in the evening breeze. He seemed entranced. Bullet holes ventilated the blades and the light from the dying sun shone through. Quin had seen the same kind of light show at carnivals using colored paper moving in front of a lantern.

Quin sat his horse beside the man, waiting patiently in growing friendship. He had nothing better to do than help watch the mesmerizing blades circle through the dusty evening.

Kiowa was quiet for a while before he finally acknowledged Quin's presence by nodding toward the other end of the street. "Horse in corral at livery."

That was a fine bit of tracking, even for a skilled man used to doing it. "How did you find that out?"

Kiowa shrugged. "Horse has start of split hoof. Needs iron shoes." He glanced at Quin. "Thought all whites put iron shoes on horses."

Shaking his head, Quin tried to explain. "The horse was Connie's pet. She didn't want to hurt him with shoeing or branding. She wants him all natural."

The man's look was uncertain.

Quin tried again. "Like a favorite dog."

Kiowa's nod was slow, his expression flat as a plate. "So, she keeps horse to eat? Why? They have many cattle—pigs and chickens. Is strange."

Sometimes, Quin was slow on the uptake. Maybe his momma dropped him on his head when a youngster. He did know Kiowa's humor wasn't all that funny, even if dog wasn't just another meat source to certain populations.

"Do me a favor?" Quin said. "You know the house where Connie and her mother stopped?"

When Kiowa nodded, Quin continued. "Please go and keep watch. If Macrae would kill his partners, three women won't slow him down much. Don't be afraid to use your rifle to prevent that."

Kiowa's stilted English and accent disappeared. "You're telling me I can kill a white man? I'd be chased clear to Mexico."

Quin's level gaze met the Kiowa's. "I'm asking you to protect those women like your life depends on it. Gather some friends if need be. You saw that camp, same as me. We don't know why Macrae staged all that, or what's on his twisted mind. All we know of him are the results we see. I don't think he'll pull anything, but we can't take that chance."

After giving Quin a long, slow look Kiowa left at a trot. Watching him leave, Quin felt a little more relaxed. He let Red drink at the tank below the windmill, and then turned toward the livery.

An older man was lighting a lantern hanging from the livery door when Quin stopped in the opening. As he dismounted a different man approached, the light from the lantern reflecting the badge on his vest as he walked toward them from across the street. Both men gave Quin friendly, but wary attention.

He nodded to them with a smile and decided to throw the skunk through the church door while he ground-reined Red. "Good evening, gentlemen. I'm looking for the horse thief that put that black stallion in your corral."

The hostler glanced at the sheriff and then back to Quin, all pretense of friendliness gone. "That kind of talk could get a man shot around here. You got any proof that's a stolen horse?"

Quin thought of the badge stuffed in his pocket, but was still determined not to use it. He grinned before answering. "Nope. But the man who claims to own him can take it up with me anytime. My name is Quinlan Barrett. I'll be around a while, or at least until the question of ownership is settled."

The two men exchanged glances before the sheriff stuck out his hand. "I'm Tom Fallon. You from up Kansas City way?"

Quin nodded as they shook hands. "A few times."

"Heard of you." Fallon nodded toward the hostler. "This here's Fred Curry, my occasional deputy."

Recounting the story of the stolen horse took a few minutes. By the time he'd finished telling of the bodies found on the trail, both men were muttering curses under their breath.

Sheriff Fallon looked at the hostler who shrugged without saying anything. Fallon said. "I don't have any jurisdiction outside of town, and not much here. So it's either a deputy US Marshal or the Army's problem, neither of which will be any help right now. We did have a deputy marshal staying here, but he left a month ago."

Quin described the fake Mexican Chico and his compadres. "Seen anyone around like that?"

Fallon shook his head. "They could be in the new part of town and we'd never know it. Can you prove anything against those men, other than being lazy and stupid—not helping when you needed them?"

"No, I can't." Quin said. "But smart money puts them with Jonas Macrae."

"Well, I don't know what you're wanting to do." Fallon pulled his hand down a long face. "There are killings and shootings every day in the new part of town. I'm usually just the cleanup crew. The best I can do is try and keep the lawlessness from spilling over to the old town. All the original people live on this side. The new part is all saloons and whorehouses. They operate cheaper than Joplin because we don't shake them down for fees and taxes, so there's a steady business."

Fallon shrugged. "If they want to kill themselves off, I'm all for it and won't stand in the way. Maybe your friends will go that way and not be a problem. That's a salty bunch up the street."

"There's one place you might see them," the hostler said. "It's chancy, but you never know. We have a dance at the Pavilion on Saturday nights. That's on their side of town. Everyone gets all fancied up for that. Even the ladies of the evening get gussied up for it. A truce is in effect. No guns or range clothes allowed in the building. Your men might show up. The dance is tomorrow night if you're interested."

A vision of Connie in a gown crossed his mind for a moment. And then he put it away. "You know Dave Pinder and the D-P Connected? They have a small ranch west of here."

"Heard of him. Never seen him." Fallon gave him a curious look.

"That horse belongs to Pinder and his daughter. They didn't brand him because he is a pet. If you'd do me a favor? Shoe and feed him, someone will be by to pick him up. I'll pay you for it."

"I don't know." Fred shook his head. "I feel like you're in the right. But far as I can see you both have staked a claim on that horse. There's no proof of ownership and no papers. The other man had possession. You take all this to a judge and he'd probably tell you to flip a coin for it."

Quin reached into his pocket for his dwindling stash of money. "Well, he doesn't have possession now, does he? Ownership is not going to be a problem. And Fred? Put a little something extra on those shoes in case that horse gets away again. Maybe a great big X. I ain't that good a tracker."

~ * ~

A local eatery served a decent supper and he tried to do it justice. Black coffee and apple pie made him loosen his belt a notch or two...alright three.

The woman filling his coffee cup was a friendly sort until he tried to get information from her. He described Jonas Macrae, hoping she'd seen him. "Have you seen anyone looking like that? Calls himself Macrae?"

She gave him a hard look. "Mister, about every other man that walks through that door looks like your description. We serve food here. We don't post letters, leave notes for the lovelorn, or sell information. You'll have to find him on your own."

Her voice softened. "On the other hand, you're spreading around that this man is a horse thief. Yeah, I heard it already. We're honest folks on this side of town and work for a living, so there's no reason for him to be here. They serve food in those fancy places uptown. Not good food mind you, but most are too drunk to notice. If your man left a horse on this side of town, it's because Fred has a Winchester and hates horse thieves. Your man won't be back until he wants the horse."

Well, that was straight enough and made sense. He thanked her for the education and rode through town at a slow walk looking in windows and scanning the people bustling around the boardwalks. One billboard offered free food and companionship to poker players—like that wouldn't be a distraction. The cardinal rule of gambling, other than don't do it, is never bet against the house. And never let the girl who works for the house sit on your lap feeding you cheese and wine while you're doing it.

He'd found the horse, so in a way his job was over. Well, Kiowa found it. Letting a killer get away with murder rankled a bit. But, more than likely, he could get over it if he tried. He didn't know the murdered men, they were thieves in their own right, nor have any desire for revenge. It was only supposition about who the murderer was, although that was a bet he'd put money on—cheese and wine excluded.

Some people he knew would say he no longer had a dog in this hunt. That pretty much described his mood. He suddenly felt adrift, like he'd just been fired from a job with no place to go. There had to be a record book somewhere about the trouble caused by having no place to go and nothing to do. But he did have a ranch to look at. There was that.

Leaving the lights and sounds of the gambling district wasn't difficult, there was no pull in that for him. Riding toward Irma Baker's house was chancy in the dark, especially being unfamiliar with the trail. He found a likely spot under a tree, staked Red on a patch of grass, and spread his oilcloth on the ground. Using his saddle for a pillow, he wrapped in a blanket against the night chill and figured to sleep that apple pie away. The memory of those murdered men prompted him to sleep with gun in hand and rock under the blanket so he wouldn't sleep too sound.

Chapter Twelve

The Baker home didn't look much better in the morning light than it had last evening. There were shingles missing on the roof and one corner of the porch sagged. It looked like a groundhog had burrowed around the rock foundation holding it up. Quin knew from experience that groundhogs and porches are like beavers and trees. They just can't help themselves.

Kiowa sat on a trimmed log someone made into a bench, eating from a tin plate. He didn't look up when Quin straddled the bench, watching him eat a moment. The pie Quin had the previous evening was long gone, leaving his stomach grumbling.

"You know?" Quin said in a reasonable tone. "A good man like you could sure earn his keep around here while on guard duty. Limber as you are, I bet you could get on that roof and replace those shingles real easy. Kind of pay for your meal. What do you think?"

He stared at Quin a moment, gravy dripping from his chin. "I'm an Indian. Don't know why white men build a house that falls down. Tepee never fall down."

"Yeah, it just blows away in the wind." Quin sighed and shook his head. "Kiowa, you speak better English than me. I've heard you. So, how about you stop with the broken, poor Indian reservation talk. You probably speak more languages than most folks ever heard."

Kiowa smiled and wiped a sleeve across his mouth. "Maybe we're both playing at something we're not."

Before he could respond to Kiowa, the swish of a skirt gave him warning. Connie stood next to him holding a plate piled high with eggs and fried potatoes. In her other hand, she held a steaming coffee cup. He was starting to like this girl again.

"Can I sit with you?" Her voice was all butter and honey as she handed Quin the meal.

"Sure." He glanced toward Kiowa. "Don't forget that roof."

Kiowa was up and away like a shot. Quin doubted if he was looking for a ladder.

"What an odd man." She watched him walk away a moment, setting his empty plate on the porch before her gaze settled on Quin. "I need to apologize to you for yesterday. Seems that's all I do lately—apologize. A lot has happened that I'm not used to seeing, and I didn't react well. I'll admit to being protected and more than a little spoiled, and I am truly sorry."

A little spoiled? His spoon made music on that metal plate. Finally, he met her gaze. "It's alright. We haven't known each other long enough to gauge reactions or make judgments."

"Thank you. That's quite generous of you." Connie gave him a tight smile. "Did you find Satan?"

That was a question that might take several hours, a preacher and covey of medicine men to answer with any degree of accuracy. He decided silence was the best road to travel.

She kept trying to look under the brim of his hat to make eye contact, so he re-settled it to a better angle—meaning he took it off and set it on the log, which he should have done in the first place. His mama had at least tried to instill politeness and some decorum in his manner. Tried was the key word.

"Well?" Her voice was going past politeness into hostility.

Quin said. "Kiowa found him. Being a certified detective, I'll naturally take all the credit for it. He's just a paid employee. The last I saw of him, your horse is well taken care of and in a corral at Fred Curry's stable in town."

Her expression was more curious than mad. "Why didn't you bring him back with you?"

She was dressed differently today, and he hadn't seen her pack a bag. The fresh smell of lilac came gentle on the morning breeze. He was sure his fragrance wasn't so alluring, unless one really liked smelling like his horse blanket.

"Well," Quin said in a mild voice. "There is still a small question of ownership that I discussed with the local sheriff. He doesn't see proof of ownership either way—something I warned you about. The other man did have possession. Also, the hostler needs to shoe him this morning. Seems he has the start of a split hoof. Your horse could have used some iron on his feet."

Color crept above her collar and he saw just a hint of temper in her eyes. He figured her true nature was about to come back and braced himself. Instead, she surprised him again.

Her smile turned soft and her voice softer. "How can I help, Quin? What can I do to fix things? I don't want you to dislike me."

Well, that confused him and he threw out the only thing he could think of. "Well, there's not a lot to worry about there, but you know...there's, uh...how are you fixed for dresses?"

"What? Dresses? Not too good. I had to borrow this one." She chuckled, picking at the material before her gaze pinned him to the bench. "Why?"

Quin tried to recover. "Well, we've found your horse, so...if you want to celebrate, there's a dance tonight in town. Some place called the Pavilion. Seems there's one every Saturday night. If you would like to—"

"You're taking me to a dance?" She stood up straight. "I don't have anything to wear. How can I...?"

They were having trouble finishing sentences. Quin interrupted. "When I rode into town, I noticed a dress shop. With the number of...well, *women* in town, I'm betting they can fix you up quick. And of course, I'd need to buy a suit...."

He was talking to her back as she streaked toward the door of the house, muttering in languages he didn't understand. Women.

Her voice echoed around the clearing before she went inside. "Kiowa, saddle my horse!"

The clearly startled warrior and man killer peeked around the corner of the house. Quin didn't know what shocked him worse, that Kiowa was holding a hammer and bucket of nails, or that he'd become domesticated. The man looked embarrassed. Quin didn't know he could show that either, but there was surely red tinges around his brown face.

A half-hour later the women were riding toward town, chattering like magpies, two in the wagon and Connie astride her pony. Quin hung back to talk to Kiowa. Once again, he tried to hand the man a gold piece, and he waved it away.

"What's going on with you, Kiowa? You used to like my money."

Gone was the stilted English. "You're a good man, Quin. These are good people." He eased himself in the saddle a moment, looking uncomfortable. "There is a girl I want to marry. The horses from those dead men will go a long way toward the bride price. Gold is no good for this."

He continued. "The Territory is not a good place to raise a family. Too much killing, too much anger. Tribes are mad at the whites and mad at each other. Too many people bumping shoulders with those they don't like. Many tribes don't get along and there is no peace. I'd like to work for you at the D-P, and bring my wife there. I could build a home. Maybe you could help me with that?"

If pigs were flying, the surprise wouldn't have been greater. "Well, neither of us has been invited to the D-P. What makes you think I'll be there?"

A smile split Kiowa's face. "I said you're a good man. I did not say you are smart. You're caught by that girl. You just don't know it yet."

There were several arguments against that notion, but none that held water. Besides, it took two for that sort of thing and he was pretty sure that wasn't on Connie's mind—dance notwithstanding. They'd talked some, that was all. Just because a girl is excited about a dance, doesn't mean wedding bells are pealing. But then again, the weighty thump of fat pigs hitting the ground echoed through his mind. Everyone knows pigs can't fly.

"Alright, let's say for one crazy moment that's true." Quin gave Kiowa a curious look. "Any ranch can use a man that's good with horses."

An idea was jumping around in his muddled mind. In some dimly lit circles, it might even be called a good idea. He decided to try it out. "Kiowa, the way I see it there's going to be shooting trouble over that black stallion. It's unavoidable. We know where the horse is, but there is still the matter of ownership, and a man getting away with stealing it. Something like that blows up and innocents get killed or wounded. That's not the ending we want."

Kiowa nodded, watching Quin with an intent expression.

That seed was taking sprout, and the idea growing to fruition. Quin continued. "I figure if I take the horse, Macrae will try and stop me even if the hostler and town sheriff don't shoot me. I'm sure Macrae has someone watching. The same goes for me if I hear he's picking up the horse. I have to stop him from doing that. On the other hand, if that horse were to disappear there'd be nothing to fight over."

Kiowa's eyes got big as Quin continued. "Now, that's a mighty fine horse. I'm thinking it would make your bride price complete, don't you think? Maybe along with a couple of gold pieces?"

"No gold." Kiowa shook his head, but a slow smile was starting to form. "And I'm not stealing from a future boss." He gave Quin a long look. "Am I?"

Pulling out his tally book from his saddlebag, Quin started writing on a blank page. "Don't think of it as stealing—well, not right away. That comes later. For now, you're trading horses for your bride."

Quin let him think on that a moment before he continued. "You're a pretty good horse thief, right?"

Kiowa was back to head shaking, giving Quin an owlish look.

"So, if a month or two down the road your future father-in-law's prized black stallion goes missing and winds up back in the Pinder corral, that would even things out in the end. Wouldn't it? Kind of a full circle?"

"Sort of a horse trade?" Kiowa's head shaking turned into a slow nod.

They were matching grins as he handed Kiowa a couple of gold pieces from his shrinking supply, along with the paper. "Now you take this money, you might need it for something. This paper gives you permission to take a black stallion with a star forehead back to the Pinder ranch and its rightful owner. It may take a while to deliver it, maybe a couple of months. On the way, the horse gets extra training from your father-in-law and you get a wife. I'd be pleased if the horse got branded D-P along the way."

Kiowa glanced at the paper, and then his gaze sharpened. "This paper is signed Quinlan Barrett, Deputy US Marshal."

Quin shrugged and then smiled. "That it is. Most people can't read my chicken scratch. You continue to surprise me."

"You are a devious man, Marshal." Kiowa said.

Quin reached across his saddle and shook hands with Kiowa. "Keep that marshal business under your hat or I'll make you a deputy. There's no surer death sentence than that. We're friends. Call me Quin like always. Now, back to the horse. I figure about dark tonight will be a good time for horse trading. From what I was told, most everyone will be at that dance."

"I owe you for this." Kiowa said softly. "Plenty."

"Well then, don't forget that roof." Quin continued. "And the porch could use a rock or two under the corner. Might shoot that whistle pig if you see it. Get some pitch and soak a piece of wood, then light the end on fire. If you throw it in that hole, the groundhog will come fogging it out of there. Don't burn down the house."

Kiowa glanced over his shoulder, frowning at the house.

Quin grinned at him, his payback for a poor joke complete. "You got all day."

Trying not to laugh at Kiowa's expression, he spurred Red toward Hard Times.

Chapter Thirteen

There was a different feel to the town when he arrived. In the few hours he'd been gone they'd decorated the outside of the Pavilion with a red, white, and blue paper banner that challenged fickle weather—a gamble the heat wouldn't stir up rain and wind in biblical proportions or the wrath of the Baptists to ruin the decorations.

After a visit to the water trough, Quin tied Red to a hitch rail and then settled next to Fred in a wobbly, cane-backed chair. "What's a man do for a bath and haircut around here?"

Fred pointed toward a building a few doors down. There was no sign, but a line of men stretched to the end of the street. He replied with a pensive voice. "That's a bath house. I'm not sure they understand what that means. I ain't seen them throw out any water yet, and they been at it a couple of hours. It's share and share alike. And if you're thinking of the horse trough under the windmill, forget it. The last dummy tried that got lead poisoning because it's near impossible to get the soap out of it."

Neither choice appealed to Quin. "Miss Connie is expecting me to look presentable tonight. I'd hate to disappoint. Any ideas?"

Fred's glance seemed neutral, but Quin didn't know him that well. "I got hot water on the stove in back. You can borrow my razor if you want. That'll be a start in the right direction."

The water was hot and after seeing the notches in Fred's straight razor, he sharpened his own on a strop of leather hanging off a stall. He must have done a good job with it because Fred borrowed it.

Pointing out back toward a jumble of boulders, Fred said. "There's a spring back there. You better get in and out quick, or you'll freeze off parts you may need tonight."

The spring-fed limestone pools come from deep underground and it was shoulder deep. Walking in, Quin swore it had ice floating on it but that's the way limestone springs are. There was a good flow to the water, and it carried the suds away down a little creek. Fred was right...he didn't linger in that water. Some clean clothes from his saddlebag and a curry brush for his hair and he felt like a new man. Parts of him may have been frozen beyond repair.

Quin found the hostler in front of a mirror trying to work over his face. "Fred, you going to the dance?"

Carefully removing the blade from his throat, Fred said. "You think I'd miss a chance of seeing every young galoot around here making fools of themselves? It's better than a carnival, and right up there with a tent revival."

Quin stared at him a moment. Something was wrong with that comment, but he wasn't going to dwell on it. Fun is where you find it. "Just so you know, along about sundown the ownership of that black horse is going to be cleared up."

"Good. I've been expecting that." Fred gave him a level stare. "So, if I was to leave him tied up...say, outside the fence next to the trees it might help things? I was thinking of hobbling him on a nice bit of grass over there. He's bothering the mares."

"If that's a problem, run him into that pool of water." Quin knew Kiowa took pride in moving around unseen and was an expert horse thief. It might be an insult if stealing the horse too easy. On the other hand, it would be something he could remind the tracker about, time to time.

Quin continued. "Now if that's settled, I need to find me a store-bought suit."

Fred settled back into his chair. "Mercantile at the other end of the street. Got all the clothes you need."

It was his kind of store. A man stood outside the door eating a can of peaches with his knife. A good part of it was on his beard and he'd be attracting flies soon. Just inside the door were saddles and bridles from workaday to fancy. Some of the leather and riatas displayed were the finest Spanish workmanship he'd seen in a long time.

At the back of the store you could buy a rifle off the rack, pistols and knives from the counter, and shovels and picks to burrow into the ground—and top it off with enough molasses and jawbreakers to tame any sweet tooth. There were eggs stored in jars and lime water. He'd heard they kept for a couple of years that way, but was never brave enough to try them.

And clothes. Inside another room full racks of all manner of clothing were hanging on display. A portly woman with a cloth tape measure draped around her neck held court in that room. She had on a bright-flowered bonnet stuck full of pins. He'd heard of pin cushions, but it looked as if she made her own rules.

A young man walked out of the room wearing skin-tight pants and polished black knee boots you could see your reflection in. A blue coat with brass buttons completed his Prussian military look. Although popular in Mexico, he might get a dubious reception here. If the man bent over, Quin was sure the pants would split...but he did look dandy. Maybe he could stand in a corner. Or hang from a hook like a flower basket.

The woman raised her eyebrows at him as he walked up to her. Quin pointed at the man leaving the room. "No."

Her laugh jiggled her frame from head to toe as she appraised him. "Most assuredly not." Her hand gripped his in greeting. "I'm Sadie."

"Well, Sadie." Caught up in her good humor, he gave a short bow over her hand. "I have a lady meeting me at the dance tonight. Can you fit me into something not too embarrassing, maybe a suit of clothes that won't get me beat up if I walk down the street?"

Sadie's gaze never left his as she chuckled, retrieving her hand. "Of course. Nothing but the finest for the beau of Miss Pinder. I saw her next door with her mother and Irma Baker. I'm sure glad you folks showed up. Irma was about to waste away mourning the loss of her son. Now, she's showing a little life. That's a good thing."

Poked, prodded, and measured for a few minutes, he felt like one of those pet dogs kept for show. It was an experience he didn't want to repeat. He was more of a cattle dog.

Finished with the preliminaries, Sadie commented. "Now, come back early this afternoon and I'll have a suit ready for you." She handed him a low-crowned, black top hat and walking stick with a silver knob on the end. He figured that knob was fake, but it did look solid.

"This will finish your look," she said. "You'll be the most elegant man there. And be sure to wear these boots. The soles are soft and perfect for dancing or fisticuffs."

"Fighting?" Quin gave her an amused look. "That wouldn't be polite."

Sadie gave him an appraising look. "Wouldn't be a dance without it. Besides, you'll have the prettiest little chicken there. Lots of weasels around looking to make her into a hen."

The pushing and pulling had him turned around like a pole-axed steer. "What do I owe for all this?"

"About fifty dollars should do it," she said in a calm, business-like voice.

His look must have betrayed him, along with trying to hand all the clothes back to her. He could buy half a horse for that. His savings were dwindling fast.

"Now, look here young man." Sadie scolded. "We have a dance every week or so. This is an investment. You need all this. Make a good wedding suit, too."

Consulting his money belt and finding the proper fare, he paid the money. There was a chair close to the door and he sat a moment. He knew the tactic. Want to brand a calf? Run him around in circles to get him confused and tired, then drop him. He was going to rest a bit.

Sadie studied him a moment as he sat, no longer smiling. "Mister Barrett, I've seen a good many men."

When he grinned at her, she colored up some.

"I'm worried about you," she continued. "When you think no one is watching, you change. You've a certain look about you. I'd say it's the look of a gunman—and we've too many of those around here, but I don't think that's it. I get the feeling you're more dangerous than most people see. It's like you're trying to be something you are not, and trying to hide what you are. Since I'm a friend of the Pinders, that concerns me."

"You're the second person to tell me that." He balked at having people try and dissect his reasons for doing anything, or judge his mood by outward expression. Curiosity got the better of him. "So how does a gunman look, Sadie?"

She gave him an innocent glance. "Well, not like you. At least, not exactly. I see them all the time, swaggering up and down the street, daring anyone to challenge them. But you're different. I see two people when I look at you. It's like the tale of two wolves, perched on your shoulders. One is good and one is evil. The say the one who wins is the one you feed the most. Which are you feeding, Mister Barrett? Which one will win the day?"

Her gaze was steady on his. "And to answer your question more directly, it's the eyes. Most look for the manner and the gun and that helps, but no. It's the eyes. Connie tells me you're a gentle man and seem to hate violence. She thinks you talked that Macrae fella out of kidnapping her so you wouldn't have to fight. You need to let her in and see the real you. I'm betting that horse thief wanted no part of what you had to offer. And I'm glad of that. A woman needs a strong man and often she doesn't know it." She pointed with her thumb over her shoulder. "This is a suit for such a man."

Well, now. That threw water on his campfire. There's a difference between a gentle man and gentleman, though he'd never claimed either. The dangers in the grass lands of Kansas and Oklahoma were no different than navigating deep water and pounding seas. One can die anywhere by misstep or misfortune. And that seemed to be in his future. He guessed it was the price of living in interesting times.

Quin's voice was somber when he finally addressed Sadie. "I'm aware of Miss Pinder's opinion of me. Unfortunately, honesty seldom factors into someone's opinion of another."

Her hand stopped him as he rose to leave. She searched his eyes a moment. "You keep a lid on those wolves, young man. Don't let them out unless you must. She might not understand."

"And if I have to?" He inclined his head to her and then shrugged. "I'm not sure there's any control over that."

"I'm sorry if I've dampened your day." Sadie said, stepping back. "It wasn't my intention."

Giving her a wan smile he said. "Good humor is like the warm water that runs on top of a dark, cold river. It's easily swayed, sometimes misdirected, but comes back just the same. You have a good day, ma'am."

Chapter Fourteen

Stepping out of the mercantile and lost in thought, three ladies accosted him.

Connie stepped close. "Quin, I've heard there's a good café just down the street. Let's have a late lunch. There's no food served tonight at the dance, just punch."

He had an idea that a little punch, bolstered with stronger spirits, would take away any thoughts of food. But he was hungry. He gave a little bow. "Yes, ma'am."

"Ma'am? I thought we settled that?"

Given her volitive nature, Quin gave her a cautious look. "Not yet we haven't. I'm not sure what to call you right now."

She didn't take offense. Instead she smiled and took him by the arm, leading the way. "You'd better figure something out, because we need to talk."

Like most men, he knew those last four words coming from a woman's mouth were signs of trouble. Quin decided to tread lightly, not knowing where this trail would lead.

After the meal of beef and potatoes, covered in a light brown gravy, they lingered over coffee and pie until almost time to go get dressed for the dance, she to the dress shop and he to the mercantile. From there it would be a short walk to the Pavilion. A few people moved by staring in the window of the cafe as Quin and Connie looked out. Some of the men stopped and gawked before moving on, giving Quin an embarrassed nod to show they didn't mean any disrespect. He didn't blame them. She was that kind of pretty.

He waited patiently, watching with studied indifference while she fidgeted on her chair. She finally got around to what she wanted to say.

"Quin, you know there will be a lot more men at the dance than women. Some will have ridden miles to attend." She looked at him like he was a difficult puzzle.

"I expect they will." His reply was cautious. "This may surprise you, but I have been to a dance before."

"Okay, that's good. But there may be some who will challenge you to let me dance with them." She still watched him with a skeptical look.

"Really? A challenge?" He studied her a moment. "Most western men are polite about such things. Are you telling me this in case some past or present suitors might show up? Just so you know." He raised his hand up to interrupt her denial and pretended to think it over. "I do believe in dancing with whomever brought you. I've heard that rule bandied about, and it seems fair. But then, it always comes down to the lady, doesn't it? You should do whatever you think is right."

"I like to dance." Her comment came like a warning, delivered with a smile.

He grinned and nodded. "Me, too. I'm betting there will be a few ladies I can dance with while you're enjoying yourself with your suitors."

"I don't have any...." Her gaze sharpened. "You'd better not dance with any of those girls from up the street."

He knew a good many girls of dubious morals would dress for the occasion and attend. If they should get lucky and grab the interest of someone, it would be their ticket out of a miserable life. He didn't blame them for trying.

"How can you tell where all the girls are from?" His smile seemed to fuel her temper. "Or, for that matter—maybe some of your suitors have already danced with those girls. Are they tainted, having touched them?"

Watching expressions change on her face was an education. Taken with the correct frame of mind it was fun if he didn't get too close to the flame and get burned.

"I swear, you are the most—" She gathered her handbag, flouncing about on her chair preparing to leave.

"Look, you're not being very clear. It's hard to tell what you're after, or what you want my response to be." They were standing by then, and he held her by both arms. "Connie. I don't know what's cooking in that head of yours. You never seem to come right out and say what you mean. You'd rather lead me into saying it. We're going to a dance. Have fun."

Her glance was unbelieving. "So, you don't care if I dance with other men?"

When you're surrounded, sometimes you must take a chance to break free. He was tiring of the repartee, and was never good at innuendo and veiled messages.

His sigh was long before he answered. "That depends on a lot of things. Let's cut to the chase. We've known each other less than three weeks. You're a beautiful woman and I've fallen under your spell. Can't help it. Not trying too hard to get away. But I'm looking for a partner in life, not someone I have to worry about what they're doing every minute. How you act and what you do is up to you and what you want to be. This is not a complicated process."

She stared at him a moment, mouth slightly open and eyes wide. When she started to say something, he kissed her. And then kissed her a little harder. After a quiet moment of staring at each other he linked his arm with hers and patted her hand. This was a victory. He'd discovered a way to make her stop talking. Ever mindful of her knee, he guided her toward the door.

"May I escort you to the dress shop, ma'am?" He asked.

"Still with the ma'am?" She smiled at him as she gripped his arm.

"A regrettable slip."

As they gained the boardwalk, quick footsteps followed through the doorway. Seemed the two chaperones were still with them. If the giggling was any sign, they were quite entertained.

~ * ~

"Sadie, are you sure about this suit?" Quin tried to look at himself from all angles.

The changing room at the mercantile consisted of a sheet draped over a wire stretched between two walls, sealing off a corner of the room. The mirror was polished metal and made him appear fat or thin, depending on his distance. When he left the dressing area she smiled and handed him the hat.

Sadie nodded, looking satisfied. "Very handsome. I'm sure all the ladies will agree."

"Not sure about the hat." Quin gave it a skeptical look, running fingers around the short brim.

Her eyebrows rose. "Trust me."

"I don't know you that well." He held the hat, once again looking at it from all angles wondering how it would look on his head. His regular Stetson hat was comfortable. This...?

Her shrug sent set off a wave of motion. "So? You trust a preacher to speak the Word? A cardsharp to steal your money? A sheriff to keep the peace? You don't know them either."

"Well...that's a little...."

"Wear the hat." Her tone bordered on anger.

"These cuffs have ruffles." Quin complained.

With a long-drawn-out sigh of the afflicted, she handed him the silver-headed walking stick and reached up to set the hat on an angle. "Get the hell out of here."

Tom Fallon met him on the walk, giving him a once-over. "What's with the hat?"

"It's all the rage." Quin replied. "You should get one."

With a chuckle, the sheriff continued walking as Quin paused and then stepped inside the Pavilion. When you walk into a saloon or dance hall, you're hit with cigar smoke, clinking bottles on glass, whiskey breath, and emotion from the crowd—some pushing merriment, some anger.

The Pavilion was a different world. A three-piece string band spread soothing music to the room. Nobody was dancing, but considering the voluminous dresses worn by some of the women, he wasn't sure they could, or that anyone would get close to them. Tables lined the walls, leaving the floor clear in the center. The floor looked like brown polished ice.

There was hope for a livelier affair in the two men sitting off to the side tapping their feet impatiently and swigging beer. With impossibly large sombreros and drooping mustaches, and looking like an artist's rendition of Mexican Banditos on the cover of a dime novel, they sat holding a trumpet and guitar awaiting their chance. He was sure most of those attending were waiting for them to take the stage.

A voice startled him. "You'll need to check your gun."

It took him a moment to recognize the man by the door. His hair was slicked down and his mustache waxed into points. Quin had stepped into a costume show.

"Fred?" Quin asked, trying to keep the laugh from his voice.

"No guns allowed at the dance." Fred's reply was solemn and measured.

Holding his coat open so Fred could see he was unarmed—well, except for the derringer in his boot. Quin shook his head. "I didn't bring my pistols. So, what's with the towel over your arm?"

"Sadie said it was all the style for a doorman." His gaze traveled to Quin's head. "What's with the hat?"

Quin began to view Sadie as a puppeteer like he'd seen in a circus—pulling strings and having a ball with the outcome. Some people liked to do that—Thaddeus Finch of the Livestock Association came to mind.

A pretty girl in a simple dress interrupted them. "Fred, where's Tom? He's supposed to meet me here."

Quin's gaze finally found Maria Pinder and Irma Baker holding court. The men talking to them parted as he walked up to the table.

"Where's Connie?" Quin asked.

Maria Pinder looked puzzled. "She came ahead of us. We thought she was with you."

Pivoting on his heel, he made for the door. She wasn't in the ballroom or they'd have seen her. Maybe she went back to the dress shop? "Fred, have you seen Connie?"

A gunshot sounded from down the street. They paused a moment. It wasn't an unusual occurrence. But still....

"Nope," Fred continued after a pause, still glancing down the street. "She hasn't come in here."

They stepped outside and saw a man running toward them. He stood winded a moment, bent over at the waist, before he spoke to Quin. "You that detective?"

"I'm not a detective." Quin felt an uneasy knot in his stomach.

"Right." The man nodded. "The marshal's been wounded. He sent me to get the detective. Said you'd have on a stupid-looking hat."

They found Fallon sitting with his back against a wall, holding a wound on his side. Pulling his shirt out, Quin was starting to check the wound when Fallon stopped him.

"That Macrae fella, the one you had trouble with? Saw someone that looked like him and some other men pushing and pulling a woman into that boarding house. I couldn't see who she was, but she didn't look like a saloon girl. There was several men and it was taking all of them to do it. When I yelled at them, one of them threw a shot at me."

He pointed across the street, and Quin reached for a gun he didn't have.

"Here. Take mine." Fallon said, grimacing in pain. "I sure as hell don't need it."

Quin sprinted across the street, checking the loads in the Schofield, hearing excited questions following him. Those soft-soled boots were still digging in when he went through the door.

Chapter Fifteen

There was a man behind the counter when Quin ran into the hotel, but he didn't need to ask directions. The scream from upstairs was all he needed.

Connie. Still fighting.

He didn't pause when he got to the room. His boot opened the door and the splintered frame hit a man in the face who stood too close.

A frozen tableau met his gaze as the man tumbled to the floor and lay still, a splinter stuck at an odd angle from his head. Connie stood in a corner, on the far side of a bed, holding a water pitcher she'd been swinging at someone. Her dress was torn, one sleeve hanging, while rage colored her face. That was the moment he knew. This was the woman to walk beside him. All the times he'd seen her mad? It was nothing like this.

One man stood out of her reach while turning to look at Quin. Chico and Macrae stood in the center of the floor, eyes shadowed by the lamp burning above them, back lit by a window with faded curtains. Curtains? Strange what imprints on your mind in times of stress.

The pistol he'd borrowed from the sheriff pointed squarely at Macrae. The man appeared pale with glittering eyes, but with the light, it was hard to tell.

Both men had pistols in their hands but seemed undecided about what to do with them. They'd been surprised when he busted in the door. They were caught between pointing their pistols at him or Connie and knowing if they moved at all, Quin would be shooting. Indecision was not a good mantle to wear in times like this. A floorboard creaked as someone shifted their weight.

Keeping everyone in his field of vision, Quin spoke in a tight voice. "Why are you doing this, Macrae? I warned you. Did you think I was fooling?"

"No, I didn't. It's a gamble." Macrae shrugged. "And I'll still win. Once again, you're outnumbered. As for the why of it? Look at her, Barrett. Look at that woman. She's the most beautiful thing I've ever seen. Like something just out of reach. You ever do that? See something pretty and all you can think of is making it your own? She got under my skin, and I'll have her before the day is done."

The man had moved enough Quin could see his eyes. No matter how animated the voice, Macrae's eyes were dead...reptilian, more void of life than the fly-specked wallpaper surrounding them.

The man continued in a truculent voice. "I will have to break her first. Maybe killing you will help with that."

Quin's breath came even and soft, his body relaxed behind his pistol, discounting the outlaw's rhetoric as desperation. "We went through this already, Macrae. It's not going to happen. Now I don't want to take a chance of Connie being hurt, even by accident. It's not much of one, but you have one chance. If you holster that pistol and leave now, you get a head start. Maybe you can get to the Territory before I catch you. Maybe you make it somewhere else. But know this. Even if you get away, you'll be staked out on an ant hill in a week, I guarantee it."

Macrae glanced at Connie and Quin almost fired. But a gunfight in a small space was suicide. Bullets have no conscience and don't care who is innocent, or who is not. They travel through walls and flesh alike, and will take anyone in their path. If he started shooting indiscriminately, Connie could get hurt. He needed an edge.

Macrae laughed. "You're telling me she's not worth the risk? Are you blind? For a nobody, you sure threaten a lot. And once again, you're outgunned and all you do is talk. You trying to trade her for something again? I already got the horse, and now I have her."

"You should pay attention, Macrae." Quin's voice was slow and soft. "Think this over. This is how a bad day ends. You started with nothing and you'll end with nothing...but death."

"You talk a good fight for someone always trying to avoid trouble. I think you're yellow through and through." Macrae's lifeless gaze turned feral, teeth bared in a wolf's snarl.

The man at Quin's feet stirred and got a boot for his trouble. Using that distraction, Connie took the opportunity and broke the pitcher she'd been wielding over the head of the man in front of her. The man stared at her in amazement before crumpling to the floor, his pistol bouncing on the bed. Those porcelain pitchers used in boarding houses were not dainty in structure.

Quin shouldn't have glanced at her because when he looked back Chico was pointing his pistol at Connie.

Macrae laughed. "Why, I think we've won this round. Now you drop that pistol or my friend Chico will shoot her. Just to wound her, mind you. Like you said, this day isn't over. We can stand a little blood to get a piece of that."

One thing was running through Quin's mind. Chico was a tinhorn. Probably thinking he had all the advantage; the outlaw didn't hammer back his pistol. Guess he thought the threat would be enough.

Macrae grinned maliciously as his pistol started coming up.

Quin didn't aim, never had in his life. His first shot took Chico in the head. He crumpled like a sack of potatoes. A surprise shot from Connie took Macrae in the shoulder, who backed up dropping his gun. Quin flinched, half expecting the pistol to go off when it hit the floor. Through the powder smoke he'd been aware of Connie grabbing the pistol from the bed, but hadn't expected her to use it. He kept his gaze on Macrae.

Quin shook his head. "Four want-to-be horse thieves drugged and killed in their sleep, Macrae. Think we couldn't figure that out? Good or bad men just out for a lark, I don't know. We'll never find out. Two of you dead here already, and we'll be hanging two more. Being around you is like picking at a scab and watching the pus run out."

"There's three of us alive. Ain't you going to hang me?" Macrae's voice was tight with pain.

"No." Quin said. "You I'm going to kill."

Macrae's eyes were feverish. "I had to have her. Don't you see that? I saw her one day out riding. When we came for the horse, you messed it up. All I wanted was her. I didn't care anything about the horse, the men could sell it and take the money."

Macrae backed up against the wall holding his shoulder. His gaze turned to Connie. "It would have been...it would...."

Before they could react, Macrae turned and leaped through the window, taking the glass and frame with him.

Quin went to the window and looked down. Macrae lay in a tangle of wood and glass, wrapped in a dirty curtain. It was a two-story drop. He shook his head. Guess Macrae thought it was better than hanging.

Turning, Quin accepted an armful of weeping Connie and held her while she trembled. It was a chancy deal since they both held pistols and didn't seem disposed to give them up. The acrid smoke in the room watered their eyes. It was hard to breathe from clutching each other so hard.

He caressed her hair as they we clung to each other. "You alright?"

She nodded against his chest. "I will be."

His whisper was inordinately loud since the gunshots were still ringing in their ears. "If anyone asks, I shot him. Simpler that way. You don't want a reputation as a gunslinger. There'd be no end of people coming against you."

Her giggle was a little manic until she got it under control, and then the hug got tighter. "Whatever you say, Quinlan."

The two men still alive stirred after a few moments. He stripped their gun belts and handed them to Connie. Both men looked sick as they stared at Chico and the wall painted with is blood. Maybe they were thinking of a trial for kidnapping and attempted rape. Both were bloody and holding their heads. The one who stood by the door pulled the bloody splinter from his head, looking at it with a blank expression before throwing it on the floor.

"Alright, boys." He got them to their feet. "Now, drop your pants."

One of them spoke. "What? There's a—"

The man's pants dropped around his ankles when Quin took out his pocketknife and cut his suspenders.

Connie spoke to the man. "You were going to rape me? Probably kill me? Now you're bashful?"

Quin grinned at her. It didn't take her long to recover.

They got to the stairs and the men hesitated, wondering how to navigate down the steps with their pants around their ankles. She solved the problem with a firm push to both.

They tumbled into a heap at the bottom as Fred came rushing in carrying a shotgun. He gave the men a startled glance. "What happened to their pants?"

Quin said. "Didn't have shackles. You ever tried to run with your pants around your ankles?"

"Just once." Fred snorted. "Didn't know she was married. Heard the front door slam and dove out the side window. I'd a broke my neck if that bedroom wasn't on the ground floor."

"Macrae just did the same thing out the window upstairs. I expect you'll find him crumpled up in the alley."

Quin couldn't believe the outcome. There were so many ways things could have gone wrong in that upstairs room. Once again he'd proved the axiom...better lucky than good.

Sheriff Fallon was leaning against a wall when they went outside, with the girl from the dance tending to him. He had a hole at the top of his hip, just above the bone. The wound bled a lot and painted her arms red up to the elbow, but she was determined and had it under control. Fallon was going to owe her a dress. The town sheriff would be sore a while, but barring infection, he'd recover.

He knew all about infection, but didn't offer the man his nurse. Reversing the new Schofield, Quin tried to hand it to Fallon and thank him for its use.

"Keep it. It's a fine gun and I have more." He laughed at Quin's expression. "This part of town has several killings a week. It's usually my mess to clean up afterwards. Another month or so and I'll have enough hardware to start my own gun store."

"Too late." The young woman shook his arm. "Your retirement starts today. We have a home to build and kids to raise. You can't do that if you're all shot up."

"Sounds like your future is all laid out." Quin laughed and then nodded. "Well, thanks for the pistol. It does have fine balance."

Fred was organizing men to march the limping captives to jail, and none too gently. If the locals did not lynch them, the first judge they saw would see they were hanged.

"What about that man upstairs and the one in the alley?" The desk clerk had a hand on Quin's sleeve.

Quin shook him off and grabbed him by the shirt. "You saw those men drag this lady upstairs?"

The man nodded, wide-eyed.

"You heard her screaming?" Quin asked.

The man stuttered a moment before he spoke. "Yes, sir. But what was I to do?"

"Then maybe you better go clean up the mess before I lay you beside them. Bring anything valuable or papers off the bodies to Sheriff Fallon. Understand?" Quin released the man's shirt and backed away, surprised at how much anger he felt toward a man who would forever live his life as a mouse. It didn't take the clerk long to leave. Maybe Quin shouldn't have vented his anger on him. Maybe.

The street was suddenly filled with horses and the men of the D-P Connected sat facing the boardwalk. One glance at their lathered horses and weary eyes told him they'd ridden straight here from the ranch.

Dave Pinder and Roundy dismounted and walked to him.

"What happened?" Pinder barked at Quin.

It took a few moments to bring him up to date. He made no sound while Quin explained, gaze pinned on his wife and daughter. His gaze swung back to Quin. "I told you to take care of them."

By then, Maria and Connie had Pinder by both arms. Maria spoke first. "It wasn't his fault. He did everything he could, and Connie was snatched on her way to the dance. Quin wasn't there."

"Dad," Connie spoke quickly. "You should have seen it. He broke into that room and knocked out one man. Then he shot the other two." She cast a quick grin at Quin. "I broke a pitcher over the head of the last one. The man that took me was wounded and went out the second-story window. He's dead. It's all over."

"Sounds like you got there just in time." Pinder's voice was gruff as he looked at Quin. "I'm obliged."

Quin watched Pinder's mouth twitch a moment. Maybe he wanted to smile and just couldn't do it yet. Having never been a father, Quin couldn't blame the man either way.

"Alright, that's it for now." Pinder said. "Connie, I still don't think you should have left the ranch." With their elbows locked together, the family wandered off down the boardwalk.

Quin had a fleeting thought that the Pinder women knew something secret about Dave and were trying to get him away. That worried him some.

Roundy broke in, staring at Quin. "What's with the hat?"

Taking it off, Quin brushed it a little, and then put it back on. "I'm beginning to like it. It's all the rage. Everyone will be wearing them before long."

Glancing at the men, he dug into his pocket for a gold piece. "The men look tuckered. This'll buy them a few drinks."

Roundy reached in and took the last gold piece in sight. "This will do it better." He handed them both to one of the men. "Turn your horses into the stable before you go. And stay out of trouble. When that's used up, charge the rest of your night to the ranch. You've earned it."

Quin doubted they heard all of Roundy's advice. They were heading toward the livery by mid-sentence, whooping and hollering.

They must have got Dave Pinder settled down quickly because Connie walked up to Quin, eyes bright with unshed tears as she wound down from the excitement. Sadie had materialized and was fixing Connie's torn sleeve as they stood on the boardwalk.

A small parade of people drifted back toward the Pavilion. The show was over, and for this town, a shooting was no more exciting than any other day.

When she came to him, he held her close. She snuffled into his vest a moment. "Your pistol is gouging me."

Mindful of her knee, he didn't give the answer that came first to mind. He took the second. "I still hear music, and you've a beautiful dress to show off."

"How can you...? Oh, I couldn't." She glanced at him. "And what about you? You killed two men, well sort of, and you want to go dancing?"

"Those men? More like taking out the garbage. I won't mourn their souls." Shrugging, Quin tried to explain. "If someone shoots at you and misses, do you go off and die anyway? If a rattler strike sticks on your boot, do you quit and never walk around the prairie again? You're made of better stuff than that. We keep on going, Connie. What just happened doesn't mean a thing. You deal with it and move on."

She hugged him tight. "I don't know you at all, do I?"

"Nope. Not yet. But I hope you will." He ignored the smiling people around them and offered his arm. "What do you say?"

Her smile was sweet, eyes twinkling with humor—something else he loved to watch. "I like the hat."

He stood a little straighter, thankful for Sadie's insight. "It's growing on me."

Her expression didn't change. "It makes you look like someone who can't decide if he's a bull or a heifer."

The hat went flying after the Pinder riders, caught a pocket of air and flew farther than he expected before being trampled under the hooves of the C-P Connected.

They cut quite the figure at the dance. That beautiful green dress she wore flared and twirled at the bottom. The slight bustle bounced and swayed. His soft shoes were kind to his feet. The dance got lively and loud, and he got all her attention. He wasn't sure, but he thought the trumpet player put a little something in the punch. He had that look about him. The kids were gone by then, and he didn't see any harm in it. Looked like they drank most of it themselves.

It was after midnight when he gave Connie a chaste kiss on the cheek and surrendered her to her mother and Edna. He thought Roundy was probably being fitted for something because he was leaving with Sadie. Probably needed a suit.

Chapter Sixteen

Quin spent the night in the back room of the jail. Sheriff Fallon had been whisked away by his lady friend to her house. It didn't look like Fallon was resisting too hard. Being a town sheriff in Hard Times looked to be a thankless and possibly life-ending job. No one would blame him if he didn't come back, although Quin would lay a large bet that Fallon would be on the job very soon.

The sun was just starting to filter through the back window and he figured it would be a while before Sadie opened and he could get his clothes. Unless Roundy brought them over. Quin smiled. That wizened old cowboy might have more life to him than most people thought.

"Barrett! Quinlan Barrett!" Pinder's voice carried through the building. "Get your ass out here."

Curious, and still half-awake, Quin rose from the bed, still clothed from the night before, and walked to the front of the jail. Pinder and several of his riders were fronting the building. He wondered if they practiced maneuvers like cavalry, they most always ended up in a line. His pistol belts were at Sadie's, and the Schofield sitting on the desk inside. The office was full of weapons, but he didn't grab any on his way out the door. His first thought was Pinder was still mad about Connie.

"What's going on?" Walking out to the boardwalk, he asked. "What's happened?"

"You got Consuela in there with you?" Pinder's voice was cold.

That was an accusation no man should have to make about his daughter. Shaking his head, Quin said. "Well, as a fine point...I'm out here, not in there. But no, I haven't seen her since she was with you last night. Why?"

"She's gone, damn you." Pinder drew his gun and fired.

Seeing Pinder go for his pistol, Quin was backing up toward the door when he felt a blow to his head. Slamming back against the wall and then falling to his hands and knees, he watched blood dripping onto the boards. The last thing he remembered was the riders of the C-P Connected making dust out of town.

~ * ~

Quin woke to a pounding headache. He jerked, and tried to set up, only to turn to the side and heave into a bucket by the side of the bed.

Laying back, wiping his mouth with the back of his hand, his breath came in gasps as he stared at a ceiling that moved like waves in the sea.

"Well, you're staying awake this time. That's an improvement." Fred's voice came from off to the side.

Slowly turning his head toward the hostler, who sat with a shotgun across his knees, and stopping when the dizziness got worse, Quin asked. "What the hell happened?"

Fred snorted. "Ain't no mystery. You got shot. That's the long and the short of it. If you didn't have such a hard head, you'd be dead."

"I remember now. Pinder shot me. Why in hell would he do that?" He tried to rise again, before falling back to the pillow. "He said Connie was gone. Did they find her?"

Fred stood and put a hand on Quin's chest to hold him down. "You're not going anywhere, so sit still and let me fill you in. Yes, Pinder shot you. And if it wasn't for me and Fallon, he'd have come back and shot you again every day this week. That's what this shotgun is for."

Straining against Fred's hand, Quin gasped. "Every day this week? How many days?"

"Damn it, boy. Let me finish. Pinder's been looking for Connie and can't find her. Someone took her. Every day he comes in threatening to burn the town down and shoot you again. He's got every man of his scouring the country, but they ain't found a thing." The hostler sighed, then continued. "I'm sorry, Quin. It's awful to think about, just awful. But she's gone."

"Nobody just disappears." He paused a moment, eyes narrowed against the pain, trying to take it all in. "How? What happened?"

Fred cleared his throat, glancing around the room before settling on Quin. "Best we can tell, it was Macrae. We made a gawdawful mistake, son. After we brought those two from the hotel in, they're already hung by the way, they cleaned up the body from the room. Anyway, in all the excitement we forgot about Macrae. When we finally remembered to get his body...he was gone. The fall must have stunned him, then he got away."

"Sweet Jesus. He's had her a week?" Quin couldn't stop the tears welling in his eyes, or his legs moving under a thin blanket as he tried to get up again. A wild, ugly thing was squirming in his belly...fighting to get out. Macrae. Those dead eyes. He had Connie.

Twisting, Quin turned and dry heaved at a bucket on the floor.

"You run out of stuff to throw up a couple of days ago so quit trying. Anyway, she's been gone six days." Fred's sigh was long and drawn out. "I don't know what else to tell you. We're real sorry...it don't seem like that's enough, but it's all we got. We just don't know what else to do."

Quin stared at the ceiling a moment, trying to calm his thoughts—steady his breathing and control his stomach. He realized his fists were clenching the blanket that covered him and willed himself to relax. Finally... "Get me Kiowa. Get me my guns."

Fred nodded. "I already sent for him. The man's been in a couple of times already. I think he's leery of towns in general. He's been waiting to see if you live or die. It'll take him a bit to get here. He's been camping out at Edna's place."

~ * ~

It was mid-day and Quin sat at a table eating eggs and potatoes brought over from the cafe. It was a chore, but the food was staying down if he didn't move his head suddenly.

Kiowa walked in and stood by the door with a serious expression. "You got a hard head, boss."

Quin glanced at him, nodded and winced. "Tell me."

"That man Macrae made off with your woman." Kiowa replied, with a hint of humor in his expression.

"I know that." Quin replied. "And I know you, Kiowa. You're the best tracker in the territory. What's the rest? Where are they?"

Kiowa took off his floppy hat, looking at the men in the room. His braided hair was showing some gray, making him look older. Sheriff Fallon and Fred were just coming in, so he paused a moment waiting for them to settle.

Kiowa continued, "I didn't get to take that horse. It's gone, so I think Macrae is riding it. I couldn't trail them because Pinder's men are riding all the trails, messing up sign. He has so many men out, it's hard to stay out of their way. He's riding roughshod over any strangers he sees. Any of our people who would volunteer to track for him are staying away because they're afraid of being strung up or shot like you."

Looking at Fred, Quin asked. "Did you put a little something extra on that stallion's iron?"

Fred perked up. "I did. There's a diamond notch on each hoof. I'd forgotten that. It won't matter much on dusty trails, but if the ground is moist it will stand right out. Hell, they gotta cross a creek sometime."

Everyone was looking at the floor when Fallon spoke. "We're out of ideas on what to do and have no idea what direction Macrae took. I've sent messages to the towns around here but haven't heard anything back. He's not in this town, but if he got to Joplin we'll never get him."

Fallon shook his head. "Last I saw of him, Pinder is a broken man—more like crazy if you ask me. He's getting worse every day. Maria is staying with her friend Edna because she's afraid to go home and be around him. There's something funny going on there."

Quin looked around at his friends. "Look, if anyone is to blame it is me. I thought Macrae was dead too. I can't imagine him surviving that drop."

"One thing." Kiowa broke the silence of men lost in their own thoughts. "It's foolish to try and track a horse after all this time. We'll waste too much time. I've heard some talk about this Macrae. He's friendly with a bunch of thieves that have a place down by the Cherokee Strip. There's some cutthroats and renegades took over a ranch. They're known for stealing women like the Comanche used to. When they're through with them, they take them south to sell them— sometimes clear down to Mexico. All the tribes avoid that place. I've heard the Army won't touch it."

"It's a place to start and better than nothing." Quin looked at his friend. "Do you know how to find this place, Kiowa?"

"Should be easy." Kiowa shrugged. "It used to be called Spring Valley. Don't know what it's called now, but I know about where it is."

The group watched Quin as he thought a moment. Finally he had some hope. "It's as good a place to start as any, and more than we had before. I appreciate it, Kiowa."

After thinking a moment, he continued. "Alright, here's what I'm going to do. Where's the nearest telegraph office?"

Fred scratched his ear, thinking a moment and glancing at Fallon. "Probably Joplin is the closest. If not, then over at Carthage or up to Mindenmines."

"I need paper." Fallon searched around in a desk drawer and finally handed him a tablet. Quin started writing. "I want this telegram sent to Thaddeus Finch, Kansas City Livestock Association. Tell him the badge is active and he is to start the paperwork for me to take full ownership of the Spring Valley Ranch."

"The badge?" Fred looked confused.

"You own that place?" Fallon was skeptical. "How the...? What are you thinking?"

"My thinking is there's going to be a lot of killing, and taking any of these cutthroats into custody is not going to happen. I have a special appointment as a Deputy US Marshal. That will take care of any legalities." Quin shrugged. "As far as the public is concerned, I'm going to homestead that ranch with full ownership. Any squatters living there will be removed by force."

"So what now?" Fred held up the paper, turning it side-to-side, trying to make out the writing.

"I'm going hunting." He held up his hand to stop the explosion of comments. "By myself, with Kiowa if he'll help. All of you have responsibilities here and need to stay. We'll make do on our own."

"You could take Pinder's bunch with you." Fred quipped.

"I don't think so." Quin said. "That bridge got burned."

"Well," Fallon looked around at the hardware hanging from nails on the walls. "You won't lack for weapons and ammunition."

Quin couldn't think of Connie being with Macrae a week without feeling queasy. "I figure to use a lot of it."

After the rest left, Kiowa settled gingerly into a chair. "You going to be ready for this?"

Quin stood and then decided against it, easing back to sit on the bunk. "I hate it, but I figure to leave tomorrow. If I can sit a horse, I'll heal on the way down there."

"There is no reason to hurry. You know he's already had her. You can't save her from that. Whatever he's wanting to do with her, it's already done." Kiowa watched him with a steady gaze.

Quin squeezed his eyes shut a moment before looking at his friend. "I know, but we can sure as hell put an end to it. Macrae said some things to me. He likes to brag. I don't think he'll pass her around to the men and if I know Connie at all, she won't be easy pickings."

"You're wrong, boss." Kiowa never wavered from watching Quin. "They are all easy pickings if you beat them enough."

Lurching upward, Quin almost stood before being pushed back onto his bed. He lay there, head swirling, trying to get his breath under control and not get sick again. Finally… "Thanks for pointing that out. I'm trying hard not to think about any of that."

"Well, you'd better think about it. She's going through hell right now. She's walking that path alone. You can't help her." Settling into the chair, dropping his hat over his eyes, Kiowa continued. "Just trying to get your head straight, boss. This ain't going to be a picnic. Not for her. Not for you. When we do get the women, I'm thinking the trouble will just be starting."

Quin gingerly raised his head, looking at the man. "Women?"

"I got word from a friend. Some did a sweep through the territory and they have my woman too, and several others. Sounds like they got a big trade coming up." Kiowa's voice was hoarse with anger. "You rest a day, then we'll go. We got killing to do and you ain't up to it right now."

Closing his eyes, Quin couldn't stop thinking about the nightmare Connie must be going through. His prayer was that she stayed alive long enough, stayed strong long enough, for a rescue.

He raised his head again, fighting the dizziness. "What's her name? Your lady?"

Kiowa stared at him a moment, hurt and worry showing in his eyes before glancing away. "Juana, daughter of old Running Elk in the Bear clan. If I couldn't get the bride price together, she was going to run away with me."

"Sounds like a keeper. We'll get her back." Quin stared at the swirling ceiling, clutching his stomach. "We'll get them all back."

Chapter Seventeen

Morning came with little fanfare. A brief thunderstorm before dawn dropped scant rain, and that moisture was already being dried up with sunrise. Quin was awake to see it all, getting ready for the trip. He didn't know what to call it. Jaunt, trip, rescue mission, or reckoning? Maybe the last. He couldn't face any scenario other than finding Connie alive and Macrae dead.

Sheriff Fallon talked him into taking a Winchester rifle, but not in the caliber of his pistols. The Winchester forty-four forty carried more punch and longer distance than the forty-five-caliber long colt. A strange occurrence that he knew to be true. But he had all the arsenal he needed. What was needed now was time and distance. Where he was going would be a hard ride.

Kiowa was waiting in the street with the horses. Fred came along and moved up to the porch where Quin waited.

"Why the pack animal?" Fred asked. "It's only a good day's ride down to the Nation."

A brass band was beating inside Quin's skull when he stepped off the boardwalk to check on the saddle straps. Luckily the wound was high enough on his head that his hat didn't bother it. Red nudged him, ears on point, not trying to stomp his toes, friendly for once. Did he know the mission, or that Quin was hurt?

"And then what?" Quin asked. "If she's not there, we keep going. We need supplies."

"Son, if she's...." The old man's voice faltered.

"It doesn't matter, Fred." Quin swung into the saddle, swayed a moment. "I'll find her."

Kiowa rode close. "You don't look too steady. There's an old mare in the stable, smooth gait, not too fast."

Grimacing, Quin gazed down the street to the south. He knew what the man was doing. A little goading and friendly banter to ease the moment—a chance to wait another day if he felt too bad.

"Thanks, Kiowa." He said, appreciating the gesture. "Just point us in the right direction and keep us going. I'll try to hang on."

"Quin maybe you should stop by Edna Baker's place on the way." Fred said. "Maria Pinder is still there and she might want to talk to you."

With a short nod to Fred and Sheriff Fallon, they rode away—an educated Kiowa warrior, a shot-up sometime deputy marshal, and a packhorse carrying more ammunition than food.

An hour of soft riding brought them to Edna Baker's door. They stayed on their horses as Edna and Maria Pinder came out on the porch.

"I heard you were alive." Maria said. "I thank God for that."

"No thanks to your husband. But I do have a hard head. Did you want to see me?" Quin asked.

Maria nodded. "I just want you to know I don't blame you for what happened. She was our responsibility when it happened. That's probably why Dave is so angry...so desperate." Her shoulders slumped. "But she's gone. There's nothing we can do now but pray."

"Why aren't you at the ranch?" Quin asked.

"I can't. The way things are, I'm afraid of Dave. We never got along all that well. I think the only thing that held us together was Connie. She was our glue. Now, she's gone and...."

"I'm going to find her, Maria. Have faith in that." Quin said with more confidence than he felt.

"But that monster has had her a week." Maria said. "She may be better off dead."

He glanced at Kiowa, not believing a mother would say that. But knowing why she did, the horror and sadness that lay behind the statement. Captivity was different for women and he knew it. "You don't mean that, ma'am. Connie is strong. She'll survive and I'll get her free. It'll be up to her from then on. Hopefully you'll get a chance to help her heal."

Maria looked startled. "You mean she may not want to come home? She may be too ashamed?"

"If she has the same attitude as you?" Quin nodded and shrugged, a hard knot in his stomach. "I'm no expert on the subject, but that's a possibility."

Maria Pinder sobbed and fled back into the house.

As they were turning to leave, Edna Baker called out. "Mister Barrett."

Quin stopped. "Ma'am?"

"You find that girl. Take care of her. And you kill that monster that took her."

"I'll find her or where she's buried." Quin nodded. "Macrae will be dead regardless."

Mid-morning found them walking their horses through a brushy valley. The valley narrowed a few hundred yards ahead. A wink of light reflected ahead and Quin stopped his horse. "Kiowa, what do think about those rocks ahead?"

Not answering, Kiowa dismounted, turned into the brush, and disappeared. A few minutes later a single gunshot sounded. Quin brought the mounts forward to the rocks.

Kiowa stood over a man that was trying to stop the bleeding in his thigh. A rifle lay out of reach, along with his pistol and hunting knife. The rifle had a long tube above the barrel for long range shooting, like they used in the late war.

Quin sat contemplating the man a moment, already knowing the answer. "What do you think, Kiowa?"

"He was going to bushwhack us. Clear as day."

"I wasn't...." Kiowa stepped on the man's leg and he screamed. "Stop. OK. Macrae told me you'd be coming. I was supposed to shoot you. He's got men out on other trails." The man was panting in pain. "Please, I think my leg's broke. Can you...?"

A gunshot sounded and the man flopped on his back. Putting his pistol back in its holster, Kiowa said. "Leg broke. Bleeding bad. Gonna die anyway."

"Well, we know one thing." Quin said as he watched Kiowa gather the man's weapons and hang them on the man's saddle. "We're on the right track. Macrae knows we're coming. He'll be ready for us. That's a good thing."

"A good thing?" Kiowa gave him a long look. "How's that?"

"He'll keep Connie alive. For bait." He looked around at the hills. "We'll need to keep a sharp eye out."

When Kiowa mounted, he pointed southwest. "I know a place, maybe get some help. It won't cost us much time."

By noon, Quin's stomach was growling when they topped a rise and saw a ramshackle trading post ahead. The roof was built like a soddy typically found farther west. This place was built in a cut-out in the hill, looking more like a front to a cave than a building. Hopefully no horse or other heavy animal would choose to graze on the roof. Part of the front wall was lifted on poles to make an awning, with a window to deal with customers.

The soddy was surrounded by a grove of trees, and common to the area, a cold-water spring bubbling from under a ridge of rocks and boulders. There was a fence around the spring with an opening that limited access. He could see a bucket by a horse trough and figured they filled the trough from the spring. That was smart. Horses wouldn't muddy it up, but any livestock around would foul the water, especially cattle. Cows were the dirtiest animal he knew when it came to water.

As they approached Quin could see several men congregated around a campfire. They looked like typical cowhands, except for long braids hanging from under floppy hats. Most had at least one feather stuck in it.

After watering the horses, they left them ground reined on a patch of grass in the shade. The extra horse was tethered to the pommel of Kiowa's saddle with a rope long enough to allow it to graze.

When Kiowa walked over and joined the men by the fire, they all stood and nodded, showing a deference Quin would have to ask about later. He heard the words Santana and White Bear. Pausing, he looked back toward Kiowa. Did he really know the man? More than one of the men glanced Quin's direction as Kiowa spoke to them.

Quin pushed aside the thin blanket used for a door and entered the dim interior. The sides of the store were piled high with merchandise, in no particular order. Clothes were piled on a saddle, furs lay on the clothes, a canteen with a wooden stopper sat on the floor. If he were in the market for something, he'd have to dig through the mess to find it and fight the rats for it when he did.

The right side sported a couple of tables with chairs, the back had a makeshift bar of planks laid across upended whiskey barrels. Oil lanterns swinging precariously from the ceiling gave the shadows movement and didn't penetrate the dark corners of the room. Quin's stomach lurched when he saw the woman sitting at one of the tables, attended by a bear of a man with a dirty white shirt and garters on his sleeves. He looked like a riverboat gambler gone to seed—a long time ago.

Taking a deep breath and immediately regretting it, considering the foul odor of the room, he turned to the man behind the bar. If dirt were alive, it had crawled onto this man and took root. His buckskins were too greasy for dirt to stick, but it had done a fine job on the rest of him.

The man put a glass and bottle on the bar. "Drink mister?"

Quin eyed the glass a moment. He'd been sick enough from the head wound without adding to it with whatever was on that glass. The whiskey would kill what was on the inside, but not the old slobbers on the outside. "I'm going to pass on that. What I need is information."

The man shrugged. "Everything in here is for sale. Tell me what you need and I'll give you a price."

"I'm looking for Jonas Macrae." Quin watched the man with an intent gaze.

"Ain't seen him, and that's free information." The bartender put the bottle and glass away, looking at Quin with contempt. "What else?"

Quin nodded. He was ready, nerves quiet, knowing what would come. "You're a liar. Macrae kidnapped a woman named Connie Pinder. She's the daughter of a rancher north of here. That man will probably be riding through here looking for scalps soon. I know Macrae was here because that woman is wearing Connie's dress."

The huge man stood, knocking over his chair. "You're that Barrett feller. He said you'd be along." The man grinned at Quin. "Reckon you're my meat for the day."

"If you don't mind I'll pass on that, too." Quin said.

The big man laughed. "That's too bad, because I've already been paid."

When he stepped around the table, Quin shot him with no hesitation. The man stood a moment, then slowly pulled out a chair and sat. Looking at the hole just under his breastbone, he looked at the woman. "He killed me."

"What did you do that for?" The bartender yelled, keeping his hands on the bar.

Quin looked at the man he'd shot, then back at the bartender. "I didn't feel like a wrestling match. Now, about Macrae? I know he was here, where did he go?"

The man shook his head. "That was pretty sudden, what you did. It was murder."

Pointing his pistol at the man, Quin spoke softly. "I won't ask you again."

The bartender poured himself a drink and then tossed it back. "Macrae is known around here. He came in a few days ago, traded that dress for a bottle of whiskey and took his woman to the back room. They stayed the night. Went on south the next day. That's all I know."

"Couldn't you tell the woman was a captive? She had to be fighting him." Quin had never felt the urge to kill someone as strong as this moment.

"We don't spend the night here." The bartender was backing away from Quin's expression. "We just rent the room out on occasion. What goes on ain't none of my business."

A sick feeling went through Quin. He knew it was going to happen to her, but hearing about it made it more real. He felt sorry for Connie, knowing she'd fight, knowing he'd beat her—Macrae promised to break her. A slight noise from behind made him turn. The huge man had settled into a lifeless lump on the chair, while the woman watched Quin with hard eyes.

"You want this dress back?" She asked, her voice phlegmy and hoarse. If she didn't have consumption, it would be along soon. "You can take it off me for a price."

"No," he shook his head and closed his eyes a moment. The dirt on the inside of the dress would never wash out. "You can keep it."

When he walked out of the dim interior of the hole-in-the-ground trading post, the sunlight made him squint and his head pound as he walked to the fire. Kiowa held out a rabbit leg dripping fat, and tin cup of water. Quin sat on an upturned stump with slumped shoulders and stared at the food.

"We heard a shot." Kiowa said, pushing the food toward Quin until he took it.

Quin sighed and finally glanced at him. "I didn't notice you rushing in to help."

"Just one shot, figured you were alright or dead." Kiowa shrugged with a grin. "What happened?"

Speaking around the rabbit leg, Quin said. "Shot a fat man." He glanced at his friend. "He was the second one laying for us. We're going in the right direction."

Turning to the other men, Kiowa held out his hand, palm up. The men dug around in their pockets, coming up with a penny apiece.

"You bet on me?"

Kiowa grinned at him. "Sort of. I bet you'd be the one coming out the door. There's one thing you're good at my friend. Singing and dancing ain't it." His expression turned sober. "They said the man in there likes to crush people."

"I figured. He was big enough for it. That don't mean people have to stand there and let him." He turned his pained gaze on Kiowa. "There's a woman in there wearing Connie's new dress."

Wincing, Kiowa put his hand on Quin's shoulder. "That don't tell you anything you don't already know, boss. You need to get your head around that. Save that anger for later."

"Anyway," Kiowa continued. "These boys are going to do some scouting around ahead of us. We shouldn't have to worry about any more ambushes."

They were walking back to their horses when Quin asked. "Those men seemed to show a lot of respect, like they knew you. Anything you'd like to share?"

"Well, I guess so." Kiowa nodded. "It is said that I'm the son of the great Santana, old White Bear Person himself. The people are kind of upset about his death last year. I can't think of any warrior of the tribes that would climb on top of a building and jump to his death. Santana was in prison so they figure he was killed."

Quin gave his friend a curious look. "So, was he your father?"

"Don't know. I never remembered anything like that." Kiowa glanced over his shoulder. "It doesn't hurt for them to think that, though."

"Wonder where they got that idea, you being a prince of the Kiowa nation and all." If his head hadn't hurt so much, Quin would have grinned.

"Funny story." Kiowa looked pensive, and then smiled. "Told my woman that story to impress her, maybe she'd tell it to her father and impress him. I guess she spread it around too much."

Quin tried to laugh but it died as he stepped gingerly into the saddle. "You restore my faith in the honesty of man."

Kiowa shrugged. "It's a gift, why ignore it?"

Sitting the saddle and watching the bartender and woman trying to drag the fat man out of the door, Quin commented. "Do your friends know anything about this Spring Valley?"

"Some." Kiowa nodded. "They say Macrae and his men are gathering many women to sell as slaves in Mexico."

"We're a long way from Mexico." He paused a moment. "Yours too? Juana?"

Nodding, Kiowa shrugged. "They saw her. She's alive. One good thing."

"There's a good thing?"

Kiowa smiled, booting his horse to get it moving. "Won't have to pay a bride price when I get her back."

He gave his friend a sidelong look. "You're not worried about what they've done to her...doing to her?"

"Not if she's alive. None of the women asked for this, Quin. It's not their fault."

"You're a good man, Kiowa."

"Don't tell anyone."

Chapter Eighteen

After leaving the odious memory of the trading post, they passed through grassy plains of water-starved grass and brush. They'd watched a roadrunner chasing a floppy eared jackrabbit and a covey of Mexican Quail kept pace with them for a while. Smaller and faster, the birds were more likely to run and hide than their larger and fatter northern counterparts known for bursting into flight from their hidden lair with a deep thrumming explosion of sound to scare the daylights out of horse and man alike.

Later that evening they could see a tree line in the distance. The trees offered needed respite from the sun. Hidden from the trees by a low hill, the men they met at the trading post rode out of a gulley to meet them. Only one seemed to be the spokesman. He spoke quietly to Kiowa, gestured toward the trees, then returned to his men. After a few moments, they waved and rode to the west.

Quin was tired, his head throbbing. "What's the news?"

"Trees ahead have a good camping place. There's a small creek that runs into the Neosho River. We need to rest before hitting Macrae's place tomorrow." Kiowa looked dubious as he glanced toward the trees.

Watching in silence a moment and knowing what Kiowa really meant was that Quin needed to rest, he sighed. "I take it there's a problem?"

Kiowa nodded. "Some white men are there holding captured girls."

"So, why didn't your friends shoot the hell out of them and rescue the ladies?" The sun and headache wasn't helping Quin's mood. The intricacies of dealing with Kiowa and his friends just added to it.

Holding up his hand, Kiowa shook his head. "We're too close to soldiers. If my people kill white men, even if they deserve it, they get in much trouble. They could hang just for helping or being around the area."

Quin checked the loads on his two pistols, adding a sixth bullet to each. Like most westerners, he kept an empty chamber under the hammer just on the off chance he might drop the pistol and it land on the hammer. Most folks would swear they weren't that clumsy, but a portion of those folks were shot by things not supposed to happen. It was good policy to never tempt fate.

Glancing at his friend, Quin continued. "I'm pretty sure they told you where the camp is?"

Kiowa gave him a nervous look. "I know it."

"Well?" Quin gave him an exasperated look. "Let's go see."

They heard the men well before they saw them. A woman screamed and several men laughed. Quin told Kiowa to hang back and cover him with his rifle. Loosening his pistols in their holsters and holding his Greener across his saddle, he rode into the clearing.

There were six girls tied together next to the creek. Another was being pushed around by three men next to a fire. Most of her clothes were ripped off. A couple of empty whiskey bottles told the story. The men stood watching him with their mouths open as he approached.

One was a man Quin had seen before at the stockyards in Kansas City. He'd been run off by the city marshal for causing trouble, and answered to the name of Curly.

"What the hell do you want?" Curly stepped toward Quin with a truculent sneer.

"You boys have one chance to live. If you let me arrest you, you'll have a chance. Not much of one, but still a chance. If not?" Quin shrugged. "Your choice."

"This is none of your concern, Mister." Curly was starting to get wary. "You better get out of here while you can."

Quin tapped the badge on his vest with his left hand. "You see this badge? If you don't drop your weapons right now, that means you're resisting arrest."

Curly blustered, holding a whiskey bottle in one hand and the other dropping to his holstered pistol. "So what? You're outnumbered and better back up and leave."

The Greener roared and knocked Curly off his feet, dead before his head hit the ground. More gunshots sounded, and the other men went down hard.

Looking around, Quin was surprised to see Kiowa coming in with his friends. "Thanks for the help. Your friends came back."

Kiowa stepped up and dragged one of the fallen men out of the fire. "They never left. I told them you could order soldiers away."

"And they believe that?" Quin snorted. "We still need to work on your honesty."

"Alright," Quin continued, gazing around the camp. "Same deal as before. Have your friends strip these men of their weapons and whatever else they have. They can keep the horses and the rest of it. I want these men buried, not just thrown in a gully somewhere. It's better if they are not found."

Quin walked to the girl the men had been tormenting. "Do you speak English?" When she gave him a blank look he handed her a blanket. She understood that and rose to take it and cover herself. He pulled his skinning knife and handed it to her butt first, and then gestured toward the bound girls. The girl walked away with the knife and a grateful look.

He was busy making coffee when Kiowa came back from helping to tend to the captives. "The men say thanks and think you are big chief, come to right all the wrongs in the territory. If they follow you around, they will get rich in horses and plunder."

Quin stared at him.

Kiowa shrugged. "Never hurts."

Coffee was made, but there were only two cups. The girls, most looked about twelve or fourteen, were sharing the hot liquid. Kiowa had spoken to them softly and most had relaxed.

Unpacking the roll of salt pork they'd been eating on to fry along with bread and a few potatoes, Quin commented. "Now what? I don't know what we're going to do with all these girls."

"I don't think it's going to be a problem." Kiowa said, his voice tense. "Don't make any sudden moves, unless it's to pray."

Quin glanced up to see riders coming across the creek and sighed. "I suppose we're surrounded."

Nodding, Kiowa said. "Damn betcha. Now you know why the boys left in a big hurry."

Standing with his tin cup of coffee, Quin looked around at more than twenty men. All were armed for war. Before he could say anything, the girls jumped up and began chattering to the men. Things seemed to relax after that. One of the warriors rode forward.

The man tapped his chest, giving Quin a curious look. "Name's Jason Walking Bear. From what our children say, you should be about ten feet tall with lightning shooting from your eyes and death from your hands."

"Not even close. I am Quinlan Barrett." He gestured toward the fire. "Light and set, we don't have much to offer but we'll share."

Jason glanced back at his men. "I could stay a bit." He barked orders and the girls jumped up behind some of the riders. They left in a shower of water through the creek, leaving behind two men who watered their remaining horses. He dismounted and sat next to the fire, while one of his men came and got his mount.

Quin gestured toward Kiowa. "This is—"

"I know him." Jason smiled. "Hey Kiowa, still the big chief?"

The two men shook hands. "Only in some circles," Kiowa said.

"What happened with the girls?" Quin asked. "Doesn't seem easy, stealing that many girls from your community."

"It shouldn't have been," Jason said, accepting a cup of coffee. The other men mysteriously appeared with their own cups. "The girls were at a swimming hole and those men must have been watching. A couple of older women watching out for them were beaten and run off. By the time they could get help, the girls were gone."

Quin whipped around and looked at Kiowa. "There were eight girls? How'd they get here? Where are their horses? Even at two to a horse, there should be more horses here."

"Which means," Kiowa nodded. "There were more men here, and they'll be coming back for the girls."

Quin quickly told the Cherokee about their women being abducted and taken to Spring Valley to be sold.

"Normally, we'd hear about something like that. We have a large tribe here." The Cherokee shook his head. "This we have not heard. It is a bad thing."

"I wondered about that. We should still be north of Cherokee lands. These men must have traveled north just to get away from your people. You're taking a chance coming here." Quin held up his hand when Jason tried to interrupt. "I'm glad you did and appreciate it. I'm curious, did you ride with Stand Watie in the Cherokee Brigade?"

"I did. That was years ago." Jason looked as if he tasted something sour. "At least until Pea Ridge."

"You boys weren't wrong about that," Quin said. "Although you got some bad press from it. Everybody runs from artillery. You should know that. If you're close enough, you run toward it. If not, then run away from it. Either way, you die if you don't run somewhere. I noticed there were plenty of blue coats running beside you. They were firing at their own men."

Quin's voice was mild as he glanced at Kiowa and explained. "The Union Generals said the sound of the artillery broke the backs of all the Indian Brigades fighting for the Confederacy, and that they ran away. There is a big difference between running away and retreating to fight another day."

"You seem to know a lot about that." Jason said, looking closely at Quin. "You would have been...what, about five years old?"

"Older than that, but your point is taken. My family lives up the mountain from Elkhorn Tavern. You might say we had a ring-side seat. It was talked about some, around the supper table. My father liked history lessons." Quin looked at the men gathered around the fire drinking coffee. "And before you ask, my family didn't fight for either side. They saw no point in it."

"Wish we didn't." Jason stood, setting his cup next to the coffee pot. "That war even had the tribes fighting against each other. It was a bad time."

"I could use your help." Quin looked up at the man. "If we work together, we can put an end to this."

Kiowa spoke up. "Quin's right. We're whittling down their numbers before we get to Spring Valley. But we could use some help."

Jason sat back down on the log, his men squatting beside him. "What can we do? We cannot be seen attacking white men."

"Being seen is the key." Quin nodded. "Your concern is that if you help, soldiers will come. And you're right. The answer to that is word must not get out about what is happening. Your men must not speak of this. We will not speak of this once we are done."

Jason glanced at his men and then gave Quin his attention. "I don't understand."

"My guess is that men are on the way here to pick up the girls." He looked at Jason. "They must not arrive. Bury them deep with no words ever to be spoken of it. Make sure their horses disappear far to the south if they are branded. Weapons and any money they have should be distributed among your people. If there is writing on the stocks of the weapons to show ownership, throw them in the river."

"You're saying we should kill these white men?" Jason didn't look as surprised as he sounded.

"Men who traffic in women and sell them to others?" Quin shook his head. "These are animals, not men. They won't reform if left alone. They will simply keep doing harm until they are stopped. There is no place for them on this earth."

Jason pointed to Quin's chest. "You have a marshal's badge. If we capture them and you take these men in for trial...?"

Quin shook his head. "If I take them in, they could go free and then come back to cause more trouble. A jury might not convict them. There are still strong feelings against the tribes. It is wrong thinking and will change in time. That time is not now."

"If the bluecoats come, you will speak for us?" Jason's gaze was steady.

"I will speak for you. On my honor."

The man sat thinking for a few minutes before answering. "I have some trusted men. All family, some who are fathers of the girls freed today. We will take care of this for you."

"Trusted men, Jason. This must be done very quiet. And that's not all. When we get to this Spring Valley Ranch tomorrow, the place must be isolated and cut off. There may be men coming up from Texas or Mexico to buy the captives they're holding. If this is so, these men need to be turned back—or buried. No one goes in, or out of the ranch until Kiowa and I are through. Do you have enough men to make that happen?"

"We shall see. That's a tall order, young general. Is there anything else?" Jason was grinning at Quin. "And what of the men at the ranch? The ones holding your women and others?"

Quin shrugged and said simply. "I'm going to kill them."

The Indian looked startled and Kiowa grinned. "Lightning, and death from both hands."

~ * ~

After the Cherokee left Quin sat a moment, holding his head. "Kiowa, we should pull back from the fire. If men get past the Cherokee, we don't want to be easy pickings for them to sneak up on."

"After we eat and I tend to your wound." Kiowa paused cutting meat and looked at Quin. "That blow to your head. It's changed you in some way. I don't remember you being so ready to kill people. In fact, it was the opposite."

"It's not the wound, although it rattled me some. There's an old saying. Circumstances are altered by circumstances. This war has been brought to me by Macrae. Right now, we seem to be killing his soldiers. When it's over, I'll be peaceful again. Maybe tell a joke or two. Will that make you happy?"

"Happy?" Kiowa shrugged. "Don't misunderstand me. You won't find the Kiowa among the five civilized tribes. I was educated in white man's school and have seen many things since. Those Cherokee and others will use white man ways to prosper. That is smart of them. The rest of us, the Comanche, Kiowa, and Apache? The small tribes? We fight until we die, or just fade away."

"That's touching." Quin yawned. "I'm going to roll up in a blanket under a tree. Hopefully, I'll wake up in the morning."

"In my travels, I have learned the word irony." Kiowa looked at him over his coffee cup. "Talking to these Indians about abducting women and selling them, calling people animals who do that?"

Quin shook his head, instantly wishing he hadn't. He was a slow learner. "I'm aware of the history, Kiowa. And the irony. But that's a broad brush, painting all men. All races of people have done these things. Evil has no color, no particular nation. We learn. We change. And that's enough philosophy for today. My head hurts."

Quin walked to the trees for a much needed rest, while Kiowa kicked dirt over the fire.

Chapter Nineteen

Quin woke at daylight to a raucous jaybird proudly proclaiming its victory over a hapless grasshopper. Humor was lacking due to a malicious root he'd fought all night, tossing and turning in his blanket trying to get comfortable. Curling up in a blanket under a tree was a smart choice from a security standpoint, but not a good choice for his back.

Stretching and moaning, he dropped his blanket roll on his saddle and moved toward a regenerated fire and Kiowa's coffee pot. Breakfast was sizzling on a skillet. The girls hadn't left them with much. Kiowa handed him a dented tin cup filled with coffee.

"Thanks," Quin mumbled, grateful for the black elixir that would hopefully blow his eyes open and sharpen his dull mind. The night hadn't been kind, filled with thoughts of the nightmare Connie must be going through—of Kiowa's woman Juana, and the rest of the captives. God willing, that would end today. And it would, one way or another. Every plan that marched through his head while trying to sleep had suicide written all over it.

"How's the head," Kiowa asked.

Giving his head a sharp shake and waiting a moment, Quin peered at Kiowa. "There's just one of you, so that's an improvement. The headache is mostly gone."

Using a stick and stirring the fire, Kiowa asked. "If this turns into a shooting, what are you going to do if you start seeing two of everything again?"

Quin gave him a startled look. "Oh there will be a shooting, make no mistake about that. If I'm seeing double, I'll just shoot between them."

"So, what's the plan? We do have a plan, don't we?" Kiowa scraped food onto two plates and immediately began slicing meat and cutting up the last of their potatoes.

Watching him, Quin stopped shoveling food into his mouth. "What's with the extra food? We shouldn't eat too heavy. It's not good for belly wounds."

"If we get shot in the belly, we're dead anyway." Kiowa said, nodding at something behind Quin. "Besides, we got company."

Quin turned and watched as a stranger moved toward them. Dressed in tattered homemade overalls, with one gallus missing, and a faded blue shirt, his shoes were worn down to nothing with his toes showing. One ear was swollen and trickling blood.

"Mister," Quin said. "Whatever road you've been traveling, I don't want any part of it."

As he stopped short of them, the man's voice was a deep rumble. "Would a black man be welcome at your fire, suh?"

Quin blinked at the apparition a moment and then handed the man his half-finished plate of food. "I'm kinda tan, my friend here is reddish brown, and you are welcome to fill out our menagerie of colors. The last I heard, meat and potatoes don't care about someone's skin. Please sit."

They watched as the man wolfed down his food. Kiowa handed him a cup of coffee that was drained in one gulp, and then another plate of food followed the first.

"I am most grateful for this." The man said, barely chewing as he wolfed the food down.

When he slowed down a little, Quin asked. "You look like you've been used up and rolled on. What happened?"

"My name's Ezekiel Fontenot. Zeke if you wish." He wiped his mouth on his sleeve. "I haven't eaten for two days and I'm most grateful for the meal, but I need to keep going."

"My name's Quin and this other man is Kiowa." The man stood and Quin held out a hand to stop him from leaving. "Zeke, you're in no shape to go anywhere. You're a big, strong man but you're about worn down to a nubbin."

"I been walking awhile. Lost my pack to thieves a couple days ago." Zeke said, putting a hand to his ear. "They walloped me on the head."

Glancing at Kiowa, Quin made a guess. "Judging from your last name and accent, you're from Louisiana. But more recently, I'm betting you came from the Singleton Colony? The one over in Cherokee County?"

"I did, suh."

Quin nodded. Former slaves were pouring into Kansas by the thousands on the promise of free land. Most were founding towns in northwest Kansas, but one town, or colony as they called it, was started by Pap Singleton. In Quin's experience they were good folk, keeping mostly to themselves. He didn't hold that against them. Whether Indian, German, Irish, Chinese or Gypsy—everyone was clannish, depending on where they settled.

"What started you walking this way?" Kiowa asked, cleaning the skillet with a flat piece of wood. "You can't just be out for a stroll."

"Men stole my wife. She'd gone down by the creek to pick berries. I been trailing them ever since that happened. Couldn't track at night, so I just kept coming this direction."

Kiowa and Quin traded glances. "That's exactly what we're doing."

"Are they close? Don't you know what they're doing to those women?" Zeke gave Quin a pained look. "Why are you just a'settin here, suh?"

"Well, even before we see the place we know we'll be outnumbered. Before you walked up here," Kiowa said. "Quin was about to tell me his plan."

After explaining what they knew about the ranch, which wasn't much, and why the outlaws were abducting women, which they were guessing at, Quin paused a moment.

"Still haven't heard the plan." Kiowa stood with hands on hips. "We going to talk them to death?"

"Nope." Quin said. "I've thought about it all night and can't see any other way. I'm going to ride down there in righteous glory, surround them and kill them all, every last mother's son of them."

"Everyone, suh?" Zeke's voice was skeptical.

"There are no innocents down there." Quin didn't know any other way. The downside were the cooks or laundry women if they had them—anyone not a combatant. But unless they were captives themselves, they'd stood for what was going on.

Kiowa shook his head. "That's the plan?"

Zeke stood scuffing dirt over the dying fire. "Don't sound like much of a plan, suh."

"What were you going to do?" Quin asked Zeke, anger building in his voice. "You're standing here half-starved, half-naked, and don't have any weapons—well, except for that skinning knife and walking stick."

The man looked at them. "My plan was to get my wife free, maybe sneak in at night and take her. I have no interest in killing more than I have to. As far as weapons, I don't know."

"Are you any good with the knife?" Kiowa asked.

Zeke shrugged. "It has served me well, suh. When needed."

Glancing at Zeke's scarred knuckles, Quin said. "These men won't fight you bare knuckle, Zeke. They'll probably shoot you on sight before you get close enough to use the knife."

"They have my wife, suh." His voice would break rocks. "I have no other choice."

"Well, now you have choices." They rummaged through saddlebags and came up with clothes for Zeke, along with a serviceable pair of moccasins.

"I have an extra pistol in my saddlebag, Zeke. Can you use that?" Quin asked.

Zeke shrugged, not holding his hand out for the weapon. "Never had the occasion, suh.'

"How about a long gun? I have a Winchester you could use." Quin was hoping they could outfit the man with something other than his walking stick. Three guns were better than two.

"Same thing, suh." Zeke answered. "Never had the need to use one."

"Well," Quin sighed, shaking his head. "I guess you're on your own."

Kiowa said. "How about your Greener?"

"That's not an option. I like my Greener." Quin answered. "It's my favorite."

"A shotgun would be good for me, suh. I can hit things with a shotgun." Zeke said, glancing between them.

Quin answered, exasperated. "Everyone can hit things with a shotgun. That's why I like it."

Kiowa chuckled. "You got two pistols and a shoot-all-day Winchester. How much more do you need?"

"I like my Greener." Quin grumbled as they set about saddling horses and breaking camp.

Zeke held the double-barrel shotgun, breaking it open to check the loads. "You got extra shells for this, suh?"

Shoulders slumped in defeat, Quin sighed. "Yeah, I got a bag full of extras. They're the new brass shells so if we're still alive at the end of the day, please collect them. I can trade for re-loads. And don't forget, that's the short-barreled coach gun. You have to get close to be effective."

"I understand, suh. I have used a scattergun for hunting and appreciate the loan."

"Yeah," Quin grumped. "Just don't break it."

Chapter Twenty

It was mid-morning when they arrived. Quin dug a dented war-surplus binocular from his saddlebag and watched the buildings below. Spring Valley was surrounded by steep hills on three sides, the fourth and flat side stretching out into Indian Territory. The valley itself was about two miles long and a mile wide. Too small for a large cattle operation, but Quin could see definite farming possibilities. Break it up into sections—goats and sheep, poultry, and a few milk cows. Maybe some shorthorn cattle, if they didn't have to walk far for water they'd fatten right up. He chided himself...if you're still alive, and that wasn't likely.

The ranch buildings were in the center, next to the hills. The main house was good sized, a single-story adobe with verandas on every side for shade. From their vantage point, they couldn't see into the windows. There was a barn with several pens and corrals surrounding it. Nothing looked like it was being used except for a few horses in the corral, most everything he could see needed repair.

As they watched, a man came out and pitched some hay to the horses, and then walked to the house. The horses turned up their noses and gazed at the lush, knee-deep green pastures surrounding the place. Whoever was inside apparently didn't care much for their riding stock.

Quin and Kiowa sat their horses on the hill above the buildings, while Zeke stood next to them.

"Looks like a slice of paradise down there, suh. The place has possibilities." He stuttered a moment. "I mean...afterwards.

"That it does," Quin said. "But first we must run out the varmints and rescue the fair damsels. OK, here's what we do. It looks like that small building off to the right probably used to be a smoke house and is where they have the women. We just saw a man come out of there with a stack of plates, so at least they're feeding them."

"I wish we knew how many men they have." Kiowa muttered while fingering his rifle.

"Yeah, me too." Quin said. "But it doesn't really matter. Zeke I want you to leave right now and come up behind that smoke house. As soon as shooting starts, you get those women to safety—there's a grove of trees over there that might be a good spot. Keep the building between you and all the shooting for safety."

"Very good, suh." Zeke replied and trotted off, holding the Greener with both hands, the ammunition bag bouncing on his hip.

"Kiowa, I want you to ride around and come up behind the barn. When the dance starts, we'll have them in a crossfire. Make sure there's no one left in the barn before you turn your back to it."

"Don't try and teach an old dog new tricks, Quin. I know what to do. What about the men in the house? What about Macrae?"

Quin shrugged. "We'll take them as they come. I'm counting on Macrae wanting to come out and talk a while, rub my face in it. He'll want to gloat about taking Connie, do some big-talk in front of his men before they try and kill me."

Kiowa sighed, checking the load in his Winchester. "Providing they all come out to see you die."

"You're a glass half-empty kind of man, Kiowa."

"Well," Kiowa answered. "I don't know what that means, but what exactly are you going to do?"

"It means you always look at the dark side of things." Quin unpinned his badge and polished it against his shirt. "Once I see you're in place, I'll go directly down this hill to the house and give them a chance to give up. My main objective is Jonas Macrae. He's the one I'm here for. The rest are just side items. If they want to leave, they can."

"Really?" Kiowa gave him an amused glance.

Quin shrugged. "No, but they can think that if they want. Even if they get away, I'm thinking Jason's men will pick them up."

Kiowa reached over to shake Quin's hand. "Been nice knowing you, Quin. If I'm alive when this is all done and you're not, I'll make sure Connie gets home."

"Appreciate it. Same for you and Juana." Quin watched his friend ride away to get into position. No matter how many times he ran it through his head, he couldn't see himself alive at the end of the day. They could wait to come up with a better plan, but they'd wasted enough time already. The women shouldn't have to wait another day.

He'd read it somewhere, didn't remember where. It was something about...morning is breaking, the battle before us, and an old man is a pitiful thing to see.

~ * ~

A few minutes later, he saw Zeke strolling up behind the smoke house while keeping out of sight from the main house. Glancing to his left, he saw Kiowa had left his horse and was entering the barn. Moments later, a man was pitched from the hayloft door, streaming blood from his neck to land in a silent heap on the ground.

It was time.

Quin nudged Red with his heels and let the horse pick a slow and careful path down the hill. He wouldn't have any cover, and no surprise. All he had was a dry mouth, queasy stomach, and a wish that this be over, with a dash of luck for himself. He patted his horse on the neck. "Red, try not to get shot this time."

He stopped about fifty feet from the back steps of the house and spoke calmly, knowing he was watched. "Macrae. Come on outside."

A voice came from inside, but it wasn't Macrae. "Who's asking?"

"United States Deputy Marshal Quinlan Barrett. Trot him out and the rest of you can leave unharmed. That's your one and only chance."

Men came walking from the house, more than he expected. Macrae came out last, standing in front while the rest stretched out to his sides. None had their pistols drawn, so he supposed they were expecting some sort of storybook shootout—or maybe just a massacre.

"What the hell do you want, Quin?" Macrae's sneering voice was loud. "As if I didn't know?"

"Hello, Macrae. You're looking pretty good for a man who dove out of a second story window." Quin thought a shadow moved inside. Even with overwhelming odds, it would be like Macrae to have some extra insurance. Kiowa had taken care of one, there was another in the house. "What I want are the women that you are holding for slavery set free. What I want is Connie. You bring them out, turn them loose and I give you men a head start. That's the only deal you get today."

Macrae smiled, his hand on the butt of his pistol. "You know, I might just give her back. I kept my promise, Quin. She's pretty used up. I did break her, just like I promised. But I hadn't thought of this. It would be the ultimate victory for me if you have her back knowing I broke her in for you."

"Well, then." Quin said. "I guess we have some bargaining to do."

Macrae's men were chuckling among themselves, grinning at Macrae's victory.

"It's hard to believe," said Macrae with a grin. "I've heard of men who like to have their women used by others...never thought I'd see it."

Red's mane shivered as he blew through his distended nostrils, once again proving the horse could read Quin's mind. He dismounted, giving Red a slap on the rump to move him out of the way. Using the distraction, Quin drew and started firing while walking toward Macrae. For the moment, he ignored the other men. If nothing else, he would kill Macrae.

Bleeding from a new chest wound, Macrae turned and stumbled toward the house. Quin fired at him again and missed. Gunfire had erupted at both ends of the barn lot while he was shooting at Macrae. A burning rip to his side and another to his shoulder turned Quin sideways and he took a knee—reloading the Schofield from a handful of shells in his pocket. Dust erupted in fountains around him as another bullet took his hat off.

Men were falling from both sides with the roar of Zeke's Greener and Kiowa's rifle. Finally, still firing, Quin struggled to his feet with another empty gun as the last man fell.

"It's a good thing we had surprise on our side." Kiowa limped toward him. "That was one hell of a fight."

"Are you hurt? Wounded?" Quin asked, keeping his gaze on the house and windows.

"Yeah, I'm wounded. I started running and a dog came out and tripped me ass over tea kettle or I'd have been in position sooner. Sorry. I meant to start in on them sooner to give you a better chance."

"Zeke," Quin groused at the other man. "There's some buckshot in my shoulder. Shot with my own gun. I thought you were taking care of the women?"

The man shrugged. "Well, suh. I figured they'd be safer in the building and that you might need some help."

Quin grinned at him, while holding his bleeding side and trying to not take a deep breath. "You figured right, my friend. Seems I'm always needing help."

"One feller ran inside the house." Kiowa said. "Should I go fetch him?"

"No. That was Macrae. He's my meat." Quin finished loading both pistols. "Watch the windows and doors on the house. There may be more rats inside that come running out. If I go down, you make damned sure Macrae does not get away."

Kiowa looked around the barn lot. "How in hell did we just do this? Quin, you're shot full of luck."

Still holding his bleeding side, Quin said. "It doesn't feel like it."

"And these men, suh? What of them?" Zeke pointed his shotgun at the fallen outlaws.

"If they ain't dead, shoot them. They were in the wrong business to deserve a trial."

"Not sure I can do that, suh." Zeke looked at him with a sad expression.

"Think about all of them with your wife." Quin took a deep breath, grimaced, and walked toward the house.

Chapter Twenty-One

Quin didn't know what to expect, but it wasn't this. Macrae sat at a large dining table, facing the door. His right hand lay on a pistol, resting on the tabletop. His left was pressed against the wound in his chest. At fifty feet, it wasn't a bad shot and Quin hadn't missed Macrae's heart by much. Quin glanced around quickly, seeing nothing out of the ordinary. This was too easy.

"You played hell, Quin. I never thought you'd pull your gun against so many. I guess you wanted me real bad." Macrae chuckled, the laugh turning into a cough bringing blood to the man's lips. "You're still confident, standing there with your guns holstered. I could shoot you right now."

Macrae was right, Quin should have had his gun out. It was a mistake. And there had to be another shooter in the house. "I'm thinking you're too weak to lift that weapon. I figure to just stand here and watch you die. Where is Connie?"

"Connie?" Coughing, Macrae closed his eyes a moment. "Consuela Pinder. My God, that's a woman. I knew she'd get me killed." His gaze locked on Quin's with a bloody grin. "It was worth it."

A slight noise to his left was the only warning. Macrae's gun lifted while Quin stepped to the right, palmed his belly gun and shot the man creeping down the hall. Macrae's bullet whipped through Quin's shirt, just under the armpit.

Another shot didn't come. Macrae's pistol lay on the table, held by a limp hand. His only sign of life was his eyes, filled with malevolent light, tracking Quin's every move.

Kiowa came busting through the doorway. "Quin, you alright?"

"Yeah." He pointed at the man crumpled in the hall. "If he'd come from my right side, I wouldn't have got him. My belly gun was already pointing at him when I drew."

"Jesus, Quin. That was cutting it too close. You gotta quit taking chances like that. Anyway, the women are freed. Zeke's wife and my Juana were with them and are alright." Kiowa's voice turned sad. "Connie wasn't there."

"I suspect she's in here in the house somewhere. I'll take care of it, and let you know if I need help." Quin had an idea she'd be in one of the bedrooms down the hall. He pointed to the man he'd just shot. "You could take the trash out."

"I will. What about Macrae? He's still alive, kind of."

"He can still feel pain and I made him a promise." Quin had a hard time bringing up any emotion, gaze locked on Macrae. "Find a hill of red ants, there's plenty around. Cut him so he bleeds. Stake him out on it. The vultures can finish what the ants start."

Kiowa's voice was a moment in coming. "Jesus, Quin. You sure...?"

Quin's voice turned hard. "Do it."

Kiowa dragged the dead man out of the hall by his heels, head thumping over the sill of the doorway, and then he returned with Zeke and they took Macrae away. Macrae's gaze was locked on Quin's until he went out the door.

Quin felt an urgency to find Connie, but dread made his steps slow and methodical. He found her in the first bedroom, tears burning his eyes when he stopped at the threshold. "Connie?"

She was on the floor, slumped against the bed. Her right hand was tied to the frame. Dressed only in a dirty white chemise, her dusky skin was mottled with bruising, dirt, and dried blood. The once beautiful hair she was so proud of draped lifeless across her face. She did not look up or acknowledge him, just stared at the floor.

Shock held him in place a moment before he rushed forward. Pulling his blade, he cut through the rope binding her to the bed. Her limp arm thumped to the floor. Pulling her to him, he held her tight, rocked her like a baby. He knew she was alive—at least, her body was. When she looked at him, her eyes were lifeless. He almost called for his friends to not take Macrae away, somehow he needed the man to suffer more—longer....

Gently holding her, he spoke softly. "I'm sorry I didn't get here sooner. You'll be alright now. I'm so sorry." He kept repeating the litany, trying to believe it himself.

Minutes later a soft knocking at the door got his attention. "Sorry to intrude, suh." Zeke said. "This is my wife, Mattie. Let the women take her, suh. A bath, some clean clothes and food might make all the difference. She needs to rest."

He nodded to the soft-eyed black woman coming through the door with another woman, he assumed it to be Juana. Gently they took Connie by the arms and walked her out of the room. Quin remained sitting on the floor, leaning against the bed, and staring at the wall opposite them.

Zeke came and sat beside him, putting his hat on the floor, running fingers through short-cropped salt and pepper hair. "Don't give up hope, suh. She's alive. Beaten and broken, used up for sure. But she's alive. That's the important thing. I don't know her, but Kiowa said she's a strong woman. You hold on to that. She'll need your help and we'll pray for her. Maybe it will be enough."

Quin glanced at his new friend, sighing, and wiping sudden moisture from his eyes with a bloody hand. "Thanks, Zeke. I appreciate it what you're doing. I haven't known you long, but you're a good man."

"A good man, suh?" Zeke looked at the floor. "I've killed enough men today to send me to hell more times than I care to think about."

Standing and wiping his face with the back of his hand, Quin helped Zeke to his feet. "Well, they do say the road to hell should be paved with the blood of your enemies. If you get to hell before me, maybe you can kill them again for what they did."

"You do have a point, suh."

There was a well behind the house and Kiowa was busy pumping water into buckets. A fire was going, heating water for the cleanup.

"I thought y'all were taking care of Macrae?" Quin looked between the men.

"Oh, Jason Walking Bear volunteered for that job. He knew just the place. It's surprising." Kiowa continued, as he poured water into the large kettle hanging over the fire. "The other women were mostly unharmed. I guess the slavers wanted them in good condition when they were sold."

Quin looked surprised. "You mean they didn't...?"

His gaze falling to the pump a moment, Kiowa sighed and finally looked up. "I didn't say that. Slavers always sample the goods. What I meant was they weren't beaten or starved. Not like...."

Feeling lightheaded, Quin sat on a stump holding his bleeding side. "I'm sorry. I—"

~ * ~

Quin woke to a buzzing sound, opening his eyes to see a bumblebee beating itself to death against the ceiling. A breeze flapped a brightly flowered, linen curtain hanging over the window. If that bee fell on him it would be mad, stinging everything it could find. He was too tired to care.

Hearing movement in the room, he asked. "What happened?"

Mattie Fontenot, Zeke's wife, moved into view and sat on the edge of his bed. Bed? Quin started to sit up when she placed a hand on his chest and pushed him back on the pillow. "You lay still a minute. I never in my life have seen a man so shot up and still alive."

She pulled a dressing away from his side, pushing and pressing against the wound, before applying something sticky and putting the dressing back. She did the same for the buckshot wounds on his shoulder and the crease on his head.

"Can I talk now?" Quin's voice echoed his exasperation.

"The proper usage is may I," she smiled at him. "And yes you may."

He slowly turned his head to look at her. "You a school teacher?"

"Among other things. I can't believe that's what you want to talk about." Her voice chided him.

"I already asked the question." Quin said. "I'm too tired to repeat it."

"And grumpy too." She continued. "Well, according to Kiowa you have a habit of fainting when you get shot and lose some blood. That's a good thing for us, because we were able to do things to you while you were asleep."

"Do things to me?" He gave her a wary glance. "What things?"

Zeke walked into the room. "Good morning, suh. Good to see you're awake. That bullet that went through your side took some of your shirt with it, pieces of it were sticking out. We had to push a rod through your wound with a whiskey soaked cloth to clean it. That would have been painful, had you been awake."

"And," Mattie continued. "That wound on your head was infected so I cleaned it out and had to sew it together. I had to shave part of your head to do that."

Quin reached up and felt his head. "I'm feeling faint again just thinking about it. What's that sticky stuff on my head?"

Licking her fingers, Mattie replied. "Honey. It does a good job against infection and you can eat the leftovers." She gave him a hard look. "Ain't you going to ask about your woman?"

"I was getting there. I'm almost afraid to. The way she looked...." Mattie moved as Quin tried to get up from the bed. "I need to go see her...." He gave a frantic look around. "Where's my pants?"

"You been in bed three days. You don't need pants." The woman stood with hands on hips.

Embarrassed, Quin look around for any way to escape while Zeke was grinning at him. "Jesus...."

"And if the good Lord wasn't on your side, you'd have been dead a long time ago. I've seen all your bullet scars." Mattie stood with her arms folded, shaking her head. "You sure must get in a lot of trouble."

Quin held up his hand. "Let's start over. First thing, thank you for taking care of me. Second thing, how are Connie and the rest of the women?"

"That's better," Mattie huffed. "Except for Juana and me, the rest of the women scattered like quail. I don't blame them. They all took horses and we just pray they had somewhere to go. Connie is, well...."

"Is she dead?" Quin asked, slumping back into the bed.

"Suh," Zeke broke in, rescuing Mattie. "She's alive, at least her body is. Her mind...?"

Mattie continued. "Connie was so beaten, so abused...the things that must have been done to her are inconceivable. Her mind seems to have left for a while. Maybe that's the only way she can heal."

It was hard to take in, she'd been such a vibrant woman. "Well, thanks again for caring for us. May I see her?"

"She's sleeping, suh. Maybe later." Zeke paused. "There are other things that need your attention, now that you're awake."

Quin gave Zeke a wary look. "And what would that be?"

Mattie left the room as Zeke continued. "It's been three days, suh. A deputy marshal arrived yesterday and gave us this packet of papers. Mattie looked through it. Somehow, it seems you own quite a parcel of land. The question is, what are you going to do with it?"

~ * ~

Quin walked out to the front veranda, supported by Zeke. His wounded side was a dull ache, and his head felt scalded on top. Easing into a rocking chair, he watched Kiowa ride up on a paint pony.

"First time I ever seen a dead man sitting in a rocking chair." Kiowa grinned at him. "I didn't figure you'd be up for a week."

"Thanks for helping out." Quin said. "I guess I was hurt more than I thought. What's been going on in our little kingdom?"

Kiowa hooked a leg around his saddle horn and relaxed in the saddle. "All's quiet, so far. I expect things will remain that way. Jason Walking Bear and his friends are patrolling the southern boundary of your new ranch. There were some men coming up the old Shawnee Trail from Texas, apparently thinking there were women for sale hereabouts." Kiowa grinned and then continued. "Part of them are still alive and heading south again so I think that business is closed for good. By the way, Jason says this deputy thing is a lot of fun."

"Deputy?" Quin's hand went to his shirt as a chill washed over him. "Where's my badge?"

"He'll give it back, now that you're up and about." Kiowa's smile was mischievous. "It does surprise some folks, though. Usually deputy marshals are more...pale."

"Now that's not true." Quin said. "There are black marshals and even a woman or two."

"Really?" Kiowa shook his head. "I've never heard of that."

It was nice to have well-meaning friends. Taking a deep, calming breath, Quin continued. "Please thank Jason for his help and get that badge back before he starts a war."

"What are your plans now, suh?"

Quin looked at his friends. "Where are the ladies?"

"They're doing some cleaning inside." Kiowa said. "You want me to fetch them?"

"Please, and Connie if she's awake." Quin had some ideas floating around in his mind, many of them coming from his time with the Livestock Association, but lining them up to make any kind of sense was like chasing chickens through a hen house.

Kiowa returned with Juana and Mattie a few minutes later. "Connie?"

Juana spoke softly. "Still sleeping, which is a good thing. Another good thing is she is not tossing and turning, and having nightmares. She's finally resting."

Quin slumped a moment and then continued. "A lawyer in Kansas City, by hook or crook, has awarded ownership of Spring Valley Ranch to me, providing we can prove it up under the Homestead Act. I know calling it a ranch is a stretch, what I have in mind is a smaller farming and cattle operation, specialty cattle to be exact—big, fat ones. I'd be pleased if all of you would stay on, and any families you might have."

"We'd be pleased, suh." Zeke spoke up, glancing at his wife. "Mattie and I have extensive knowledge of farming."

"Good. What about you two?" He looked at Kiowa and Juana. "Will you stay?"

"Sir?" Juana's accent was very heavy.

Like most Indians, Quin was sure she knew several languages and English wasn't one of them. He held up his hand to stop her. "Please. I can't seem to stop Zeke from the habit, but don't call me sir. We are equals, here. Call me Quin."

She gave him an embarrassed smile and unleashed a torrent of words at Kiowa. After listening a moment, he said. "She says yes."

"That whole speech boils down to yes?" Quin laughed.

"Pretty much." Kiowa grinned and continued. "We would like to stay here if we can. And we have a good start. There's about twenty horses left here by the unknown parties who may or may not be buried about a mile from here. Those horses include Connie's pet stallion. He'd make a real good stud if we could keep him. We gave some horses to the ladies who wanted to leave. All the saddles and tack are here, and you wouldn't believe the number of weapons and ammunition. It's like they were expecting a war. We could outfit a pretty good bunch, which is an idea I'll run by you later."

Zeke chuckled. "Well, suh. If they did expect an attack, they didn't get the one they were looking for."

"OK," Quin said. "I'll let y'all figure things out in the short term while Connie and I recover. We'll need to brand those horses if we want to keep them. Kiowa, I also need you to send a rider to Connie's mother to let her know Connie's condition. See if she's still visiting her friend at Hard Times."

"We can do that," Kiowa responded. "We need a brand for the horses and cattle."

Quin thought a moment. He didn't know if Connie would have anything to do with the place after what happened to her, but he'd chance it. "We'll call this place the QC. I'll get it registered when I can." He glanced around at them. "Spring Valley seems a little tame after what we went through to get it."

Mattie spoke up. "Shall I enter that in your journal? I've been keeping it up to date for you with all that's going on. I must say it is very detailed. You've had an interesting road through life so far."

"You can write?" Quin asked.

"Better than you." Mattie said with a snort. "I wasn't real sure what language it was written in at first."

"Quinlan." The voice interrupting them was hoarse, coming from the doorway to the house. Connie stood holding onto the frame, a wan looking ghost, barely standing.

"Girl, what you doing out of bed?" A startled Mattie forgot to use proper English and started moving toward her.

Connie's attention was on Quin. "You need to change the brand. If that C stands for my name, don't use it. You don't have me, and you will not. Damn you for leaving me with that man for a week. I'll never forgive you for that."

Quin watched speechless and Connie turned back into the house. Mattie and Juana were close behind, helping her back to bed. What did he expect? He looked at his friends and shook his head. "I don't know what to do."

"It's early," said Kiowa. "She'll come around."

"She's on laudanum, suh. Probably out of her head. Mattie gave it to her to make her sleep."

"She sounded pretty sane to me." Quin slumped back into the chair. "I guess I expected too much. This place is where everything happened. She'd never want to live here. I was foolish."

"Funny thing about that," Kiowa said. "Juana and Mattie talked to her. Seems like Macrae and those slavers just couldn't wait so the trail was where the women were raped. Once they got here, all that stopped. Sounds like in Connie's case, Macrae must have kept her tied up, beat on her some, and starved her. What did he say to you...he broke her? He never touched her again. Not like you're thinking. But he surely did break her. I've seen horses broke gentler."

Soft steps alerted them to Mattie coming outside. "She's asleep again. If you men want to quit postulating and pontificating on things you know nothing about, Juana is putting out a supper that smells pretty good. Y'all are invited."

When she turned and went back inside, Quin said. "Zeke, how'd you land someone as smart as her?"

"It is a mystery, suh. And make no mistake, she and Juana are hurting too. They just deal with it in a different way."

Chapter Twenty-Two

Supper over, the ladies were fixing a plate to take to Connie. Quin interceded, "I'll take this to her, ladies. If she's awake, we need to talk."

Mattie glanced at Juana and then shook her head. "It may not be the time, Quin. Maybe you should give it a while."

He took the plate and mug from their hands. "I don't see the point."

Connie was sitting up in bed when he walked into the bedroom. She hastily pulled the covers up to cover her chest as she glared at him.

Ignoring her hateful look and with more good humor than he felt, he said. "Dinner is served, M'lady. Shall you take it in bed or at the table?"

"Take it away. I'm not hungry." She turned her face away from him.

"You need to eat. You know that." He could see talking to her would be like walking on eggshells.

Her voice was soft, lacking emotion. "You don't understand. I don't want to talk to you, Quin. Just go away."

He put the tray of food on a small table, and then sat on the side of the bed. "Well, you're going to be disappointed. Why don't we start with why you're mad at me?"

Her head swiveled around so hard he was afraid she'd break something. "Five days, Quin. I waited for you to come. I prayed for you to find me. I knew my hero was on his way, the one who broke a door off its frame to get to me in that hotel. I kept telling myself I could take whatever was happening," she paused and shuddered, "if you'd just come and kill that monster.

In a voice turned hard, she said. "You didn't come for me."

He sighed, trying to find his voice. "Well, there was a good reason for that. You should know...."

She interrupted in a harsh voice. "Oh, Macrae told me all about it. He said you'd be along after sampling the girls from the bawdy houses. He said after the dance you spent the night at a sporting house and that you were so drunk the next day you couldn't get out of bed. Macrae told me all about you—a killer with a badge."

Quin stood, instinctively backing away from her anger. "I don't understand, Connie. That man did terrible things to you and yet, you believe what he tells you?"

She gave him a defiant look. "Where is Macrae? Did you kill him too?"

"Well, if he's not dead, he's praying for it. He's feeding the ants and vultures right now. Hopefully, it won't make them sick."

"You didn't come for me." Her voice was listless, a hopeless breath finding no reason to continue, fixated on one thing— his lack of action.

"What I'm trying to tell you...." Quin tried to touch her arm but she flinched away.

She screamed at him. "Get out of here."

Quin walked out into the shadowed hall and leaned against the cool adobe wall. Straightening, he started to go back inside when he felt a touch on his arm.

"I tried to tell you." Mattie was leaning on the opposite wall. "She's not ready. What that monster did to her body was bad enough. Thank the Lord we all heal from things like that. But what he did to her mind? It's like taking her body wasn't enough. Somehow he convinced her that everything he was doing was your fault. It's like she's on Macrae's side. I don't understand it."

They were interrupted by Connie, standing in the doorway. "Neither of you understand anything. I'm well enough to travel and I wish to go home. Can someone make that happen?"

"I suppose so." Quin gave a resigned sigh. Then he firmed up, excepting things the way they were. "If that's what you want, we'll see that you get there. Do you wish to go to your father or your mother?"

Connie gave him a startled look. "They're not together? How can that be?"

"Many things have happened that you don't know about. The last I knew, they were not." He shrugged. "Maybe that's changed. Are you fit to ride your pet stallion, or do we need to find a wagon? It's a day's ride on horseback, longer by wagon."

"I'll ride Satan." Her chin rose as she glared at him.

Quin nodded. "Good. I'll find someone to take you home."

Connie gave him a scathing look. "It won't be you?"

He sighed and shook his head. This was not how he thought their reunion would go. "Your mother was staying with Missus Baker the last I knew. If you go there, I can take you. I can't go to the Pinder Ranch."

She looked from him to Mattie. "And why not? Are you afraid of my father?"

Quin studied her a moment, wondering if the woman trapped inside would be worth waiting for. "You father is the only man to have shot me and lived to talk about it." He rubbed his shoulder and glanced at Mattie. "Well, except for Zeke and that wasn't his fault. When I see your father, I may rectify that."

"If my father shot you it was well deserved. When did this happen?" She looked confused a moment. "Ah, I understand. You want revenge for that. So, back to being a killer—what you do best?" Tears were coursing down her cheeks as she stared at him.

"And what was Macrae?" Quin couldn't keep the words from spilling out. "What was he?"

Connie looked confused a moment. "You were forcing him to run, he was just getting back at you."

"You mean after he stole your horse and kidnapped you? It's my fault?" He stared at her a moment, not believing what he heard. When he started to reply Mattie held her hand up. "Stop this. It gets you nowhere. But Connie? You've been lied to. You think about that."

"By whom?" Connie's rejoinder was quick, and left them with stunned expressions.

Quin recovered and spoke in a flat voice. "I guess you'll have to think about who hurt you the most. It surely wasn't me."

"That's what you don't understand. I don't want to think about any of it." Connie's voice was anguished.

"That's your choice." Quin faced her. "But just to keep the record clear, I didn't come for you immediately because your father shot me the next morning. I didn't wake up for days. I came for you as quickly as I could."

When she didn't answer, Quin continued. "We'll leave first thing in the morning. I'll see you get to your mama. After that you're on your own."

Moments later, Quin stood on the veranda facing south into the breeze. He took a deep breath and held it, slowly letting the air out and trying to relax. It didn't work.

Mattie had followed him out and spoke from behind him. "She's damaged, Quin. That's what I tried to tell you."

"I know." He turned to look at her. "I do. But it's unfair and hard to take."

Zeke came up and put his arms around Mattie, Kiowa leaned against a post. They could hear Juana rattling pots and pans inside. This is the way it should be, friends gathered on the porch after supper telling stories and swapping lies— discussing the day and hopes for tomorrow. He turned and looked at his friends. Connie should be with them.

"We couldn't help but hear," Kiowa said. "Hell, they heard that clear to Joplin. Do you need company tomorrow?"

"No. I think that would just complicate things." Quin straightened, glad to be thinking of something other than Connie. "Y'all need to stay here in case any of those idiots get past Jason Walking Bear's men. The Cherokee have helped us and we need to figure out some way to repay them for their kindness." He glanced at all of them. "It's good to have friends. I mean that."

"Is there work you want us to be doing, suh?"

Quin thought a moment. "For now, it's clean up and straighten up the house and buildings. Make things as livable as possible. We can figure out who's responsible for what later. I know the corrals need work; we'll have to haul in lumber for that."

"Other than taking Connie home and hoping she doesn't kill you on the way, what will you be doing? When can we expect you back?" Kiowa gave Quin an expectant look.

"I'll get her home, and then I'm going into Joplin to the land office. I'm hoping to re-file on this place under the Homestead Act. I don't want to ride clear to Wichita or Kansas City to do that."

Zeke gave a confused to Mattie before looking at him. "I thought you already owned the place, suh."

"According to the papers given to me, I do. But I don't really trust Thaddeus Finch. His reasoning for helping me were pretty thin. I'm thinking if I file on this place separately, it will keep him from taking over things once the homestead contract is complete."

"Do you think he'd try that?" Mattie asked.

Quin chuckled, shaking his head. "He's a Kansas City lawyer. His office is larger than some homes I've seen. What do you think? Another thing is this—the Homestead Act will only cover 160 acres. That will cover the buildings and a couple of springs close by. I'd like both of you to look around, Kiowa to the north and Zeke to the south so you can file on the rest of the land. That is...if you want to. If you decide you don't want the land after it's proved up, then I'll find a way to buy it from you."

Zeke looked at his wife and then back to Quin. "That's very generous of you, suh. Thank you. It's an opportunity I don't think we expected."

"We all deserve some peace." Quin said. "I think with some hard work and smart choices, this land will give it to us."

"I don't think homesteading applies to an Indian." Kiowa groused. "It's kind of funny, applying for ownership of land we already use."

"You have a point," Quin said. "You don't have to do it, but if you wish we'll find a way. I'm thinking that, with a good lawyer, you won't have to let them see your smiling face. We'll get it done, one way or another. Once filed, the deed is done. In five years we all show we've made improvements and the land is ours."

"And don't forget," Quin continued. "Until you can get places built, this house is yours. There is plenty of room."

"What about Connie?" Kiowa asked.

Quin sighed, looking at the door and wondering if she was listening. "I don't know. That's going to depend on her. We'll still brand as the QC. I'll file on the land under the name of Spring Valley Ranch, like the paperwork already says."

Kiowa said. "Well that should keep us all busy for a few days. I do have one other thing you should give some serious thought about, boss."

Knowing Kiowa, Quin gave him a wary look. "And that is?'

"Juana has a sister who will come to live with us. She's very pretty, a good cook, and works hard." Kiowa said.

Kiowa almost fell from the porch when Mattie hit him with a towel.

Chapter Twenty-Three

Another restless night brought the promise of a clear, hot day. After a heavy breakfast of fry bread, salt pork, and potatoes, Quin walked onto the veranda rubbing his stomach. With Juana's cooking, he might need to cut his meals down to one a day or he wouldn't be able to get on a horse. And needing a nap after every meal might cut into his work time. When he asked her about the big meals she'd just replied that she was happy to be able to cook, to be free. Quin couldn't argue with that.

Red and the pet stallion Satan were saddled and ready to go as Kiowa came up on the porch. "What about a pack animal, boss? You need supplies?"

Quin shook his head. "We'll travel straight through and should make it by this evening. Besides, Juana packed enough in a saddle bag to feed us for a week if we get hungry. That should be enough."

Zeke came out the door. "Are you sure one of us shouldn't come along, suh. Some of Macrae's people could still be around."

"It's possible, but that's the reason I want you to stay here and guard the place. Stay armed, and place some of the rifles we found by the windows and doors. I plan on hiring a couple of freight wagons to deliver supplies. It may take a few days for all that to happen." Quin stood by the horses, giving all the straps a final tug.

"Kiowa," Quin continued. "You might see to the burying of whatever is left of Macrae. I wouldn't want someone to find the remains and report it to the army. It's probably on Cherokee land, they'd get the blame and that would lead to trouble they don't need."

Giving a short laugh, Kiowa said. "Been meaning to tell you, that body is gone, boss."

Staring at the man, Quin said. "Surely that man didn't resurrect again."

"Not exactly. His hands and feet are still there…just the body is gone. You might remember that most of the girls he held were from the tribes around here. It was a practice in the old days to cut off the hands and feet of your enemy so they couldn't hurt you in the afterlife. They left those for some reason, but I'd say that body is scattered to hell and gone."

"Well, hell." Quin sighed. Some might call this settled land. It was not. The danger was real and varied. "Bury whatever is left."

"I'll see to it, boss. After the ants, it's just bones anyway." Kiowa's gaze turned to the door of the house.

Quin turned to see Connie emerging from the house dressed in homespun pants and a faded, blue shirt. An old, floppy hat with a notch in the top was set tight on her head. Not speaking, she immediately went to the stallion, mounted, and settled in the saddle. She stared straight ahead, not acknowledging anyone.

"Did I hear you were going to buy supplies?" Mattie asked. "If you do, please get us some cloth so we can make dresses and other clothes. None of our clothes are looking too good and all we have are borrowed pants."

"I'll make sure of that." Quin took his hat off, rubbing the wound on his head. The healing process had it itching like poison ivy. "Personally, I have nothing against pants. With the amount of work to be done around here, you all may be wearing them before long."

"Begging your pardon, suh. We're needing a bit of everything. This place was stripped clean of most everything useful. Unless we use pistols for hammers and rifles for fence posts, we need supplies to work with."

"And ammunition?"

"Enough to fight a war, suh."

Giving the man a sharp glance, Quin said. "I see you still have the Greener."

"It's a fine instrument, suh." Zeke gave him a slow smile.

Quin grinned at that. It was a small price to pay. The work side of having a ranch was rearing its ugly head and hopefully his savings could stand the hit. "I'll take care of getting supplies. Which reminds me."

He turned to Kiowa. "You might see if a couple of those Cherokee boys will work on the cheap keeping track of our horses. We seem to have inherited several."

"Maybe." Kiowa said. "Those boys eat more than all of us put together."

"Well, butcher something."

Mattie patted Connie on the leg. "Well, we've already said our goodbyes. Good luck to you, Connie. We love you and hope to see you back here with us." The ladies turned and moved back into the house with scant reaction from the lady on the horse.

Mounting Red, Quin glanced at Connie. "You could at least have said thank you."

"Already did." Connie's words were terse, not inviting any conversation.

Quin gave a half-salute to the men and pointed Red northeast. This was going to be a swell trip.

"Have a pleasant journey, suh."

Everyone present was aware of the tension between the two people leaving. Giving the man a dirty look, Quin dared him to smile.

~ * ~

They'd ridden a couple of hours when Connie spoke. "Quin, slow down. This horse has a bumpy gait, and the ride is hurting more than I thought it would."

Stepping off Red, he took a thin blanket out of his saddlebag and folded it. "Raise up."

Connie stood in the stirrups while he spread the blanket on the saddle.

"Now, sit." His voice was brusque. "See if that helps."

"We'll see." She gave a small sigh, gazing off into the distance. "Thank you, Quinlan. Please don't hate me."

That stopped him cold. Her emotions were like that ride in the bucket he took in Kansas City. One minute you're fine, the next minute the bottom drops out. He was expecting anger, now she seemed meek, docile. "Nobody hates you, girl. You've been through a terrible ordeal. None of it was your fault."

Her glance skipped off him like a rock. "I don't need your pity, either."

It was a slow ride after that. He rode around any stretches of ground that seemed too rough. Normally, he would ride through a gully going down one side and up the other. Now he looked for an easy way around. The creeks were the worst, with the horses lunging and jumping if there was a muddy bottom. Though mute, he could tell she was in pain.

He guided them into a grove of trees that had grown up around an outcropping of limestone and one of the many cold-water springs. There were persimmon trees, but he knew they wouldn't be good to eat until after a good, hard frost. "We'll stop here."

Connie stood in one spot when she dismounted the stallion, her back rigid and tears glistening on her cheeks. "This was a bad idea. I'm sorry I insisted on leaving."

"We all make mistakes," Quin replied. "Lord knows I've made plenty of them."

He glanced at her, standing rooted to the spot, knowing she was too sore to move. It was like she was waiting for a cramp to go away. "You need to take your pants off."

Her stricken look told him how big a mistake he'd just made. For just a moment the horror and shame painted her expression before it turned to calm acceptance. "As you wish. Since you're a man, I'm surprised you waited this long."

"Look, I know...."

She interrupted, anger spilling over. "You don't know a damned thing."

"Don't read this the wrong way." He caught her by an arm and led her over to the spring. "You're not used to riding, over and above what you went through. What you need to do right this minute is drop your pants, and sit your butt down in that cold water. It'll help. Stretch out if you can. When you're ready to get out, I'll put liniment on your legs to warm them up. It won't smell too good, but it will help keep the stiffness away. Some on your back would be a good idea too."

Hesitating, she look around the campsite.

"Connie," he said. "There are bushes all around. No one can see and I won't look."

After checking the area for snakes, although he knew they were more likely to be around warm, still water and not this cold spring, he went about making camp. He'd be surprised if Connie moved from this spot until tomorrow.

He heard a splash and yelp come from the spring. "Connie, are you alright?"

"Yes," she answered. "This limestone is slick and the water is damned cold."

He smiled. Sometimes these springs were cold enough to make your teeth hurt. After a few minutes he heard her getting out of the pool. Throwing a towel over a bush, he said. "I'll get the liniment to put on you."

"You will not. I'll put it on myself. Just set the bottle on the rock and turn your back. You're not seeing me without my pants on." Her voice quivered from the cold.

He chuckled and did as he was told. "Be sure to wash your hands after you put it on."

"I was raised on a ranch, Quin."

He spread his ground sheet and a blanket on the ground next to the fire. Bread, pork, and cheese lay on a cloth spread on a clean, flat rock. She moved toward him, holding the liniment bottle and hesitated...looking from the bed to him.

"Stop it." Quin said. "I figured you'd be better off laying down as sitting. Maybe I was wrong."

"You weren't wrong." She knelt on the blanket and then reclined, leaning on one elbow while using her other hand to eat with.

He sat a canteen next to her. "Enjoy. I'm going to see to the horses."

~ * ~

She was asleep when he returned from watering the horses and hobbling them on a good bit of grass. He covered her with a blanket. Grabbing his rifle, he retreated to the rocks. Finding a good backrest, he settled in. Other than a slight dust trail to the north that had to be freight wagons, their world was a quiet place as she slept the afternoon away.

The problem with solitude is the mind never shuts off. He wondered what Connie was walking into going home. He'd heard of things like this before. It was much like when women were captured by the tribes and then escaped. Sometimes they were not welcomed back. Not because anyone hated the victim, but because they hated the people who captured them. Some viewed the woman coming back as dirty and used. Some even suggested the captive should kill themselves. He'd seen it and heard it.

People have small minds. Many are unable to move beyond their own little slice of life, unable to fathom the way things are from the other side. Empathy was an unknown word or concept. Oftentimes unknown to the victim as well.

His biggest worry was that Connie wouldn't accept help, would hate men in general, hate him in particular, and especially reject any sympathy. Telling her he was sorry only seemed to make her mad.

~ * ~

The sun was casting long shadows when she finally stirred. Quin got up and stretched, taking another long look around before moving down from his perch in the rocks. He paused, looking at her for some sign of how she felt. Receiving a noncommittal glance, he set about making camp. Next to the rocks, there was evidence people had used this for a camp in the past, and that bothered him. He'd chance it for one night.

"I'll gather some firewood." He glanced at her. No answer. Fine.

Gathering dry wood from some of the deadfalls around, he clubbed a curious rabbit for supper. There were quail, but he didn't want to chance a shot. Going back for his camp shovel, he cleaned the rabbit and buried the remains. Hopefully doing that would keep any curious coyotes away. They generally wouldn't harm people, but could be a nuisance scurrying around in the darkness.

When he returned Connie had a small fire going in a circle of rocks next to the limestone wall. It would reflect the heat and help keep them warm. Hot days and cool nights were normal this time of year. He roasted the rabbit over the coals while frying what was left of the bread and potatoes. The juices dripping from the rabbit meat fell into the pan of bread and potatoes adding flavor.

"I've never seen cooking done that way." Connie said. "That's a good idea."

He was surprised she'd spoken. "I have skills."

With a gaze that was uncomfortably long, she grunted and returned to looking at the fire.

"Look, I know you're hurting. I get that." When he didn't get her attention, he continued. "I can see where you'd hate all men. I get that too. But most men aren't like Macrae. The good ones won't throw you on that blanket every chance they get...unless you ask them too."

He sighed. "We had a good time at your ranch. You were flirting and trying to get me interested. I was ignoring you because you were the rancher's daughter and I felt when all the fairy tale dreams were over, we couldn't be together. You had everything you wanted and I had nothing—nothing to give, nothing to offer. But for a while it was a good time."

In a soft voice she said. "Well, I guess I'm not too good for you now."

"Why? Because you were raped and beaten? That has nothing to do with your worth as a person. Macrae said he broke you. Mattie said to treat you lightly because you were broken. Are you, Connie? Are you broken?"

The first sign of spirit came bursting from her. "No decent man would want me now. Not after this. Not after what happened."

"That's only true if you accept it. If you act broken, you will be. It's all a matter of perception. Do you think I'm a decent man, Connie?"

"Yes, I guess so." She watched him curiously.

"Yep. I clean up nice and wear good clothes. I ride a nice horse and talk well, thanks to a good education from my parents. The perception of those around me is that I'm a good man." He grunted, throwing a stick on the fire. "I am not."

Her gaze was on him, showing just a spark of attention. "Since I rode away from my home in Arkansas, I've always carried a badge. What's that mean? I sometimes have to kill people, which is a contradiction. If there was a warrant out for someone's arrest for breaking the law, I was to bring them in. Most times they objected and fought. Killing men is against the law too. As a US Deputy Marshal, as a Railroad Detective, as a rep for the Livestock Association, and now again as a deputy, I've killed those men who objected. Some would say it was justified. But was it? Did I have to? No. I could have been a farmer, or worked in a store. So, I'm not a good man. But I'm not going to let that drag me down to the point I lose myself in a jug of whiskey or bottle of laudanum like some folks do. I'm going to keep trying. Maybe I'll make it, maybe not. But I'll hit the problems face on, not cowering in fear."

"So you think I'm a coward for feeling bad that I was treated badly?" Her voice was hard and unforgiving as her opinion of herself.

He'd heard once that women were a breed apart and not to be understood. Now he knew why. "No, that's not even close. I'm telling you to respect yourself. Plain and simple. Probably did a bad job of it."

After splitting the meal between them, Quin set about cleaning the pan with sand, and then rinsing it in the pool. It was dark by then and he knew they were far enough from the water that they wouldn't keep wildlife from coming to drink. With the horses watered and hobbled on grass again, and the campsite cleaned up, he backed against the rock. Using his saddle for a pillow, he glanced at her before settling his hat over his eyes.

Connie sat staring into the remains of the fire as he spoke to her. "I keep wishing Macrae were still alive, just so I could kill him again. For what he did to you, I'll be killing that man in my dreams for a long time, always in new and inventive ways. This is my fault, Connie. I should have killed that peckerwood the first time I saw him. I did not. So, the burden is mine. Let me take it."

Her stare was intense as she watched him. "It was true, then? My father shot you?"

Quin doffed his hat and pointed to his partially shaved head. "He nearly did me in."

She sighed. "I'm sorry. Once again I've misjudged things. I've always been too quick to anger."

"This time it's acceptable, Connie. Now get some rest."

~ * ~

First light saw them mounted and headed toward Irma Baker's place, chewing on cold rabbit for breakfast. After three hours of uncomfortable silence, they walked their horses up to the hitch rail in front of the Baker home. Smoke rose lazily from the chimney and they could hear conversation inside the home. Smoke and sparks rose from the chimney as someone regenerated the fire.

"Hello the house." Quin called.

After a moment of silence and then a shriek from inside, two women burst from the house, Maria in the lead. It was the quietest reunion he'd ever seen. Mother and daughter clutched each other tight and cried, finally moving toward the house.

Missus Baker lingered for a moment, her hand on his knee, gazing up at him. "Thank you, Quinlan, for bringing her home. Will you stay for the nooning?"

Gazing at the house he finally met her gaze. "No. I've gotten her home, the man who abducted her is dead, along with his men. All of you should be safe now. Anything else and I'd just be in the way, so I'll be moving on to town."

He tipped his hat. "Have a good day ma'am."

Chapter Twenty-Four

It was an uneventful ride into Hard Times. Everything looked the same. The bawdy street pointing toward Joplin still looked like a disturbed anthill with people scurrying from one doorway to another. A blacksmith was pounding the keys on a piano, trying to beat them into submission, and he was pretty sure he could hear the trumpet from the Mexican Banditos who played at the dance. Maybe they were practicing for the next one.

Sadie's store was still open when he tied Red to the hitch rail and dragged his scuffing feet inside.

"Well, look what the cat drug in, or maybe what the cat spit out. Quin, you look terrible." Sadie walked to him and administered a hug. It surprised him how much he needed it. She looked up at him. "Tell me you found her."

He sat on a three-legged stool by a counter. "I did. With a little help from my friends, most of his gang is dead and Macrae's body is scattered to the four winds." He took a little time and gave her the story.

"So, Connie is back with her mother?" Sadie set out some bread and cheese, and a bottle of sarsaparilla. "Here, this will light up your sweet tooth."

She watched him eat a moment. "What now? What's next after you've saved the fair damsel and righted the world?"

He snorted at that. His world was a ship taking on water. "I need supplies. We have a ranch with nothing to do with. There'll be three of us men and two women. We need everything."

"Not Connie?" Her voice was nearly as sad as her expression.

"She wouldn't spit on my tongue if it was on fire...so, no Connie. Can't say as I blame her much."

After spending an hour making lists, half of which Quin wouldn't have thought of, she said. "I don't have all this stuff, of course. It will have to come out of Joplin. Here's what we'll do. Let me order it, you'll get a cheaper price from me, and I'll have it freighted to you."

"How do I pay for all this? I don't think the bank will loan money on wishes and the promise of maybe having a paying ranch soon. Right now I'm long on horses and short on everything else."

She laughed. "You're right about that. The bank won't touch it, but I will. Sound good?"

"Good? I don't know why you'd take a chance and grubstake us, but I'll take it. You're a life saver Sadie."

"Don't be so sure." She turned serious. "You still have Pinder to deal with. He wants to readjust his aim and put it a little lower—like right between your eyes."

Quin shook his head. "I don't understand that. He still blames me for what happened to Connie?"

"You better believe it. Dave Pinder is the kind of person who always has to be right and everyone else is always wrong, facts be damned. His bright and shiny daughter was put on a pedestal and you let her get tarnished. Someone besides him needs to take the blame, and you're it. In his mind, you have to pay."

He nodded. "Well in a way, he's right. Like I told Connie, I should have killed Macrae the moment I saw him. But I pegged him wrong. I thought he was just a horse thief and a wannabe bad man."

"You know the old saying about hindsight, Quin. We can't read other people's minds. There is one other aspect to this. You know Connie was adopted?"

"Yes, Pinder told me. He said she was a foundling. I can't see what difference that would make?"

"Well, scratch a little deeper. Ever since Connie was a teenager, Dave's marriage to Maria faltered. All his attention fell to Connie, a beautiful young woman in his house that he's not related to. Now, I'm not saying he'd do anything about it. But you can see how it would play with his mind? And if he was already a few cards short of a full deck? You need to watch out for that man."

"That makes no sense to me." He was silent a moment, lost in thought. Finally, he met Sadie's gaze. "I'm too simple a man for palace intrigue. I'll try to avoid him."

"Good luck with that. He's got a big crew and they're looking for you."

"Well, I still have a faint hope Connie and I can get together. If I get cornered and have to kill her father?" He sighed and gave her a sickly grin. "Well, she does hate me already. Guess it can't get any worse."

"I wouldn't put money on that. Things can always get worse. If you say it can't, fate takes that as a challenge. Just remember you got friends, Quinlan."

He patted the counter as he got up to leave. "Thanks for the meal, Sadie. And the advice. You're a good friend. I'll try to not let you down."

"Advice is worth what you pay for it." She gave him a long look. "You be careful."

~ * ~

It was full dark when he led Red to the livery. Lanterns were burning at both doors and he could hear something stirring around inside. Moving through the doors, he began stripping the saddle and blanket from the animal.

"Well, hell." Fred walked toward Quin with hand outstretched. "We had peace for a while. Now we'll get lightning bolts and twisters. It's good to see you."

They shook hands as Quin asked. "So, what's the latest disaster in town? All Sadie would tell me was to watch out for Pinder."

"She's right about that. Ain't that enough?" They got Red situated in a stall with a bucket of oats, and a water trough for company. "That man's gone crazy looking for you and Connie."

"Funny that I never saw him where he needed to be. Connie is safe and sound with her mother."

"Well, that's the thing." By mutual consent they headed across the street to the Fallon's office. "He's making a lot of noise and stirring up dust, but that's about it. His threats make it a windy day, but we never see anything useful from it. Word has it that his ranch is really suffering."

A young boy came running out of the office, followed by Fallon strapping on his gun belt. "You boys had supper?"

"Nope." Fred glanced at Quin. "What's the catch?"

"There's been a shooting at the Aces and Eights saloon. That's not unusual, but the man doing the shooting is threatening to shoot everyone. I figure to spring for your meal if you back my play at the saloon. I don't want to get shot in the back. How about it?"

Quin shrugged and reached in his back pocket, pulling out the marshal badge and pinning it on his shirt. "Sadie fed me some, but I'd love to spend some of your money for another meal."

Fred ran for his rifle as the other two headed up the street. Like any place in town, it was a short walk to the saloon. Once inside they saw a man who appeared to be drunk, clutching a woman with one arm and a pistol in his other hand. He fired into the floor as they watched.

"What's the play?" Quin asked.

"I'm not used to this." Fallon shrugged. "Not sure."

Glancing at a grizzled man dressed in buckskins who seemed unconcerned as he sipped from a glass of whiskey, Quin asked. "How many times has he fired?"

The man glanced up at them. "Well, you got one dead man. There's two new bullet holes in the floor and one in the ceiling. Reckon that makes four."

"So, he has one, maybe two left...depending?"

"Hell," the man in buckskins said. "He don't look smart enough to keep an empty under the hammer. I'd figure two."

Quin moved toward the man who looked like one of the German immigrants who'd taken up farming west of town. The gun barrel wobbled as it tracked Quin. Stopping within arm's reach, he said. "How about you let the girl go. She's done nothing wrong."

"Nothing wrong? She was flirting with that damned cowboy." His accent was so strong, it was hard to understand him.

The way he said cowboy was not a compliment. And it wasn't. Most drovers Quin knew didn't like to be called cowboys. He shrugged and shook his head at the man. "Look, you're a farmer. That man you shot looks to have been a drover, or cattleman who came in for a drink and a little companionship. She is a bar girl. What do you think her job is? She hustles for drinks and anything else she can get. If you're looking for romance, this ain't the place."

The man was bleary eyed and stubborn. "I bought her drinks. She was mine."

"Now you're looking for loyalty for a few drinks?" Quin laughed. "What do you think our job is?" He pointed to Fallon and Fred, and then at his badge pinned to his vest.

"He has a gun." The German farmer was looking nervous as he pointed his gun at the body on the floor like a finger and then gave Quin a sly look. "This was self-defense."

"I doubt it." Peering over at the body, Quin said. "Yeah, just what I thought. His shooter is still in its holster."

Distracted, the farmer was looking owlishly over Quin's shoulder. Standing straight, Quin snatched the pistol from the man's grasp, leaving the German with some skin on the trigger guard and a bent finger.

"Ow." The man stood holding his hand.

Quin glanced at the girl. "What's your side of the story?"

She snorted. "This farmer comes in all the time. He's got a wife and kids. All he wants to do is feel up the girls and get drunk. By the time he's ready to do something he's too drunk and we've wasted our time. All that poor drover did was smile at me."

Fallon had the farmer's hands tied with a piggin string and was leading him toward the door. He called over his shoulder, "I'll meet you next door in a few minutes."

A couple of men walked up. "What's going to happen to that farmer?"

"You friends of his?" Fred pointed to the man on the floor.

The man gave a disgusted look toward the farmer being led out the door. "We work for the same outfit and we'll be pulling out in the morning."

Fred nodded. "Well, here's how this will go. The farmer will get a trial. If no one comes forward to testify against him, he'll get time served. If you and the young lady testify, he'll hang for killing that man. Pretty simple."

"Well, we can't stay around for that. The crew leaves for Texas at first light." One of the men said. "We'll take care of our man, bury him someplace and notify his kin. That's about all we can do."

Someone showed up with a blanket and they rolled the body in it. As they carried the unfortunate man out the door Quin said. "I am betting the soiled dove will have flown by morning."

"Morning?" Fred looked around the room. "I'm thinking she's gone right now. There's no way she'd show up for a hearing."

"So, he'll have died of natural causes?" Quin asked.

"Pretty much. I don't think we could prove anything beyond poor judgement." Fred slapped him on the shoulder. "Let's get some chow. We'll give Fallon the good news when he gets back. That boy trying to keep law and order in this town is like herding gophers."

"Herding gophers? Fred, there is something seriously wrong with you."

~ * ~

After they had supper, the trio walked toward the old town. Leaving the hustle and bustle of the gambling district behind them was a physical relief. They stopped in front of the jail.

"The offer of the back room still goes," Fallon said. "The price is right and that bunk has a hell of a lot less bugs than the hotels."

"I'll take you up on that," Quin said. "I'll be leaving early tomorrow. I'm going into Joplin to find a lawyer to draw up some papers."

"Guess you ain't been to the other end of this street." Fred offered. "We got us a new bank and a couple of lawyers. I figure they can use the business."

"That's OK by me." Quin nodded. "I can't think of anything I've lost in Joplin."

The hoof beats of several horses coming up the street interrupted them. Standing in the darkness, under the awning of the sheriff's office, they remained unseen as the group moved by. They finally rode into the gambling district.

One man peeled off from the group and stopped in front of them, sitting his horse quietly as the rest rode away.

"How's it going, Roundy?" Quin's voice was quiet.

"Figured it was you skulking around back there in the dark. I saw the light reflecting off three badges and you'd be the only extra one I could figure. You need to leave town, Quin. Pronto."

"I take it Pinder was leading that group that just went by?" Quin shook his head. "It won't help if he and his crew get drunk."

"Well, just thought I'd warn you. Pinder doesn't have to drink himself crazy. He's already there."

"Does he know Connie is with her mother? We took care of Macrae. There's no reason for hostility now." Quin sighed, knowing it wouldn't help. "You might tell him that for me."

"He'll come for you, boy. You got to know that. It ain't right, but there it is." Roundy backed his horse away from the awning. "I'll tell him. Then I'm quitting. I want you three to know that. Pinders ranch is gone...cattle and horses scattered to hell with no one around to take care of the place."

"After you quit, you might visit Connie and Maria out at Irma Baker's place. They'll be glad to see you." Quin said. "They need to know exactly what's going on."

They watched Roundy ride slowly up the street. Finally, Fred said. "Well, that was enlightening."

Quin shrugged. "Considering he's Connie's father, I'm kind of in a pickle. I guess the best thing is for me to avoid him."

"You can't do that forever." Fallon said. "You'll have to deal with him sooner or later."

"And do what? He's already shot me once. I don't see him backing up or being sorry for that."

Fred snorted. "You need to do what you do best, boy. You're going to shoot his ass and go on with your life. That's what you've got to do."

"There has to be a better way." Quin said his good nights, and went into the jail to stare at the fly-specked mosaic of the ceiling above his bunk. It was a long night.

Chapter Twenty-Five

The next morning Quin moved through the door of the jail relieved that he didn't get shot leaving the building. He easily found the Hard Times Land Bank & Loan Company, wondering how they got all that lettering on the window, and was sitting in front of the desk of Horace Morgan, Esquire. They'd finished the paperwork to open a ranch account for Spring Valley Ranch, and filing paperwork to establish the QC brand, all to be filed in court. He also put Consuela Pinder as a co-owner.

"Now," Horace said. "I understand you want to file on these sections of land under the Homestead Act?"

Quin opened his saddlebag and brought out the wad of papers he'd received from Kansas City. "While I worked for the Kansas City Livestock Association, Thaddeus Finch convinced me to take ownership of the ranch under certain conditions he said were legal and I have doubts about."

"I know old Thaddeus." Horace reached for the papers. "I think you're wise in seeking another way."

"He seemed really anxious to do a good deed for me, even pushing through a special appointment as a Deputy US Marshal" Quin grinned at his lawyer. "He was very helpful."

"Indeed. I'll just bet he was." The man was quiet as he leafed through the papers, pausing now and then to peer closely at something. "I'll check with a judge, but I suspect none of this would hold up in court. So, we'll refile just to make sure. Since we already have a description of the land in question, it should be easy."

"Actually, I need to file on three sections. I'll keep the home place with all the buildings. There are sections to the north and south that will be held by other families."

"Excellent. The powers-that-be are anxious for new settlers."

"The north section will be made out to Kiowa Smith and his wife Juana."

"Although there's legislation going through to fix this, right now an Indian can't own that land. It might take years." Horace looked concerned.

Quin shrugged. "Kiowa is just a nickname, but it's what everyone calls him so he's taken the name. The south section should go to Zeke Fontenot and his wife Mattie."

The lawyer beamed. "Sounds like a fine southern family."

"Yessir. He's southern as they come." Quin said with a smile.

"Alright," Horace was busy making notes. "I'll get all this written up and they can come in and sign the papers."

Sighing, Quin said. "Well, that's a problem. They're both real busy. There may be a question of holding the land against certain lawless elements who wish to move them off. I'm not sure they can sign their names anyway. How about I sign for them?"

The lawyer watched him a moment. "Well, since you're an officer of the law, and in the interest of sticking it to old Thaddeus, I have a better idea." He turned his head. "Myra, can you come in here a moment?"

A trim young woman appeared at the door to the office wearing a blue dress, ink on her fingers and pencil stuck in her hair. "Yes sir?"

"We have some papers to sign, along with Marshal Barrett. For just a few moments, you get to be Kiowa Smith and Zeke Fontenot."

"I'm sure we can make that happen, sir." She smiled at Quin. "Pleasure to meet you. If you'll make an X at the appropriate place, I'll sign their names. The doctors say I seem to have multiple personalities of penmanship."

He grinned at her. "You do this a lot?"

She nodded, pen and ink bottle poised. "It's hard to keep up with all the X's."

"You know," he glanced at his new lawyer. "It occurs to me this is about as shady as our favorite lawyer."

"Somewhat." The banker grinned. "But this assures he can't take what is yours. Our deal will stand the scrutiny of time and of a judge. And for what it's worth, I'm loyal to my customers and your reputation precedes you."

~ * ~

It was afternoon, and with his stomach grumbling, Quin walked toward the livery with a saddlebag full of papers. It was time to saddle Red and make a stop to see Connie on the way home. Home. It had an odd sound to it. Good, but odd.

Pausing at Sadie's mercantile to check on his delivery, he found her behind the long counter sorting buttons. "How's your day going, Sadie?"

"Before or after I knocked two jars of buttons off the shelf? At least it was better than knocking off a jar of eggs." She glanced at him with a pair of glasses perched on her nose. "Your shipment of goods should be loaded on freight wagons and headed to your ranch today. It'll take a couple or three days to get there."

"Excellent." He glanced at her. "How do they know where it is?"

She paused her sorting, black on the left, ivory on the right, brown in the middle, and gave him a serious look. "When they hire men from the owl hoot trail, the drivers and guards all know where your Spring Valley is located."

"They hire outlaws to deliver goods?" He shook his head, not believing what he was hearing.

"Sure. They pay the men a good wage, usually more than they would get from stealing the load and splitting the money with other gang members, after they would have to sell it for pennies on the dollar. And the freight drivers know all the tricks their peers might throw at them. Makes sense."

"Peers?"

"Brothers-in-arms, compadres, other outlaws, and such. You need to read more, Quin."

His next stop was the livery. Fred had his horse saddled and ready when Quin arrived. He secured the saddlebags and stepped up to Fred. "Thanks for keeping Red for me. Looks like he's fat and happy."

"That horse bites and tries to stomp on feet. Why don't you turn him out to pasture?" Fred approached on an angle, avoiding teeth on the front and hooves on the back.

Shaking the oldster's hand, Quin replied. "I'm used to him and the mares just laugh at him. Why make him suffer more indignity?"

Fred laughed. "Yeah, kinda like me. You're not going by the Baker's to see Connie are you? I think Dave Pinder rode out that way this morning."

"I am. If Pinder is there, he can be glad or mad in the same boots he arrived in." Quin rubbed the scar on his head. "I owe him a few headaches anyway."

"Now son, it's a bad thing to start fighting with in-laws." Fred was grinning at him

"That's not going to be a problem. Pinder shot me for letting his daughter be stolen, delaying me several days, causing her a lot more grief and pain than she deserved. Plus Connie hates me for waiting so long to rescue her. What can go wrong? I'll just pay my respects and try to avoid bloodshed."

"Why don't you just pass them by and avoid the whole mess? Nobody would blame you for that."

"No, I can't do that. I want it settled with Connie and Dave Pinder. I don't want to spend time looking over my shoulder wondering if either one of them will show up." Quin still couldn't think of any reason Pinder would wish him harm, even if he was crazy. And Connie? He was having a hard time figuring out just what he wanted to happen.

Chapter Twenty-Six

Quin had heard that the road to hell was paved with good intentions. But no paving stone could be worse than indecision, a malady that sometimes seemed incurable. Go or stay, fight or run away, all had equal parts of logic that resulted in a reasonable conclusion. He and Red were stopped on the trail above the Baker home while these thoughts ran through his head. Red didn't care.

There looked to be a crowd at Missus Baker's place. Several horses were either tied to the hitching post, or ground reined in the shade. He could see Roundy sitting on the porch, while a few men idled by the side of the house. All seemed uncomfortable, casting glances at the door.

It was a still day, with no wind to rustle the leaves, so the raised voices and pottery flying out a window prompted Quin to heel Red in the flanks. Their arrival to the front of the house was a flurry of dust and jingle of spurs as he mounted the porch and moved through the front door.

"What the hell is going on in here?" His voice rapped out at the startled tableau before him, the characters frozen in surprise. Connie, her mother, and Irma Baker were backed up against a counter with a table between them and Dave Pinder, who was flanked by two other men.

"You!" Pinder erupted, pointing his finger at Quin. "What are you doing here?"

"Actually," Quin was watching the two men with Pinder. They weren't drovers or ranch hands. Both had squared up with their hands on the butts of their pistols. "Missus Baker is a friend. I thought I'd stop by and check on her."

He kept his gaze on the three gunmen before him. Three, because that's how Dave Pinder appeared, just like the others with pistols in easy reach with the loops off the hammers. "Do all you men like to bully women?"

The men flinched, not liking the insult, but he kept talking. "How are you Missus Baker?"

"Well," she smoothed the front of her apron and dress. "We were fine until these hooligans showed up."

He nodded, still not moving his gaze from the men. "And how about the Pinder ladies. Are you alright?"

Connie cleared her throat before speaking. "Thank you, Quinlan. We'll be fine now that you're here."

Dave Pinder couldn't be quiet any longer. "Enough of this. I'm taking my wife and her whore of a daughter home with me. That's my right."

At the word whore, Quin almost drew and fired. His desire was clear enough that the two men with Pinder almost followed suit, and then relaxed. "It looks to me like the ladies don't want to go with you...."

Maria Pinder interrupted. "That's correct."

Quin continued. "And the only people here of low regard are you and the two cur dogs with you. That about right?" The last thing in the world he wanted was to start something. The room was too small and shots fired could go anywhere. "You get a one-time offer to leave standing up and not carried out on a board. Your choice."

"You think we're scared of you?" Pinder blustered. "Hell, I shot you once and can do it again."

"Your shot was full of dishonesty and betrayal. I was unarmed, and thought you were a friend." Quin noted the surprise on the faces of the two men behind Pinder.

Pinder flushed. "It wouldn't have made any difference if you'd been armed."

Quin was moving as Pinder finished the sentence. Drawing his gun while stepping forward, he clubbed Pinder's hand as the man tried to draw, then hit him over his left ear and dropping him in a stunned heap on the floor. When he turned, he found the two gunmen standing with arms raised and facing the door.

Kiowa's voice filled the room. "I think we got this covered, boss. You want me to shoot these peckerwoods, or take them out back and spank them."

"What are you doing here?" Quin asked.

Keeping his attention on the Pinder man, Kiowa answered. "Ranching is boring."

"You'd only been at it three days."

"Still..." Kiowa smiled and gave an eloquent shrug. "There's more excitement in following you around."

"Alright," Quin said. "Take these boys outside. I assume you've already taken care of the rest?"

"Roundy and Zeke have them."

"Zeke is here, too? Who's taking care of the ranch?" He wheeled around to look out the doorway.

"Jason and the boys are keeping watch. I promised them a horse or two."

Quin sighed and pointed to Pinder. "Drag this outside and tie him up."

The roar of a shotgun from outside startled them. "It's alright, suh. One of these boys got jittery. He's all settled down now."

As the two men started to walk toward the door, Quin held his hand out for their guns. They complied, one of them saying, "We didn't know the truth of things. Sorry."

Quin nodded. "Next time pick a better man to back. Or get an honest job. I hear freight lines are hiring guards."

Pinder was waking up so they got him to his feet. He was wobbly, so they had to help him walk.

"Head hurt?" Quin asked, but didn't get an answer—didn't expect one.

Missus Baker and Maria were coming out the door of Edna's home. Maria paused, with her hand on Quin's arm. "Gently, Quinlan. Don't give up on her."

Inside, they faced each other. Connie still leaned against the counter, apparently rooted to that spot. He leaned against the table, watching her expression for a hint about how to proceed.

"So, what happens to my father?" Her voice was tentative.

He shrugged. "Attempted murder of a federal agent. Assault on a federal agent."

She gave a hint of a smile. "I didn't see any assault."

It was Quin's turn to smile. "He was thinking about it. In any event, he'll be out of your mother's hair for a good while. I'm thinking that's a good thing."

"It is, although she'll be lonely at the ranch. She won't know what to do."

He nodded, leaning against the table and folding his arms. "Well, I know a good lawyer who might could help her sell it."

"And us? What about you and me? Could you ever want someone like me?" Her voice was shaky.

"Someone like you? My God, Connie. You'd be a catch for any man you decide to be with." Somehow he was holding her in his arms. "You're a beautiful young woman with life before you. Don't low-rate yourself."

"My own father thinks I'm a whore, because of what that man did to me."

Quin held up his hand. "Stop right there. Your adopted father has no sense. Does your mother say that? How about anyone else? Juana or Mattie? Do you think any of those girls we let loose would come back and call you that? I don't think so."

"You don't know...."

"Stop saying that. You're right, Connie. I don't. Only you and Macrae know what went on while he had you, and his body is scattered so many places I'm not sure God can find enough to send to hell."

She stood mute, tears running down her cheeks.

He hugged her tight for a moment. "I'll help with what I can when I can. That goes for all the others. But right now it's up to you. Did he break you, Connie? Are you broken?"

~ * ~

Quin left her, walking outside with a sizable lump in his throat, wondering if he'd lost. Irma Baker and Maria looked at him and he shrugged. When they started inside he shook his head. "Give her some time."

The Pinder crew sat on the ground. They weren't tied up, but their holsters were empty. The two from inside stood next to them, nervously watching everyone. Dave Pinder lay on his side, trussed hand and foot like a calf waiting for branding. Kiowa and Zeke stood patiently by their horses.

He turned to the ladies and pointed to Pinder. "Maria, do you want anything to do with this man?"

She strode to the edge of the porch. "No, I do not. He was never a delight to be with and now he's just crazy."

Moving to his horse, he took out his daybook and a blank arrest warrant. "Well, I guess Mister Pinder will be a guest of the state for a while, although which one I don't know."

"Be easier to shoot him." Kiowa looked distastefully at the bound man.

"Yes," he glanced around at everyone. "But then we've got all these witnesses, so we'd have to get rid of them...where does it all end?"

Kiowa responded mildly. "Just a thought."

"So," Quin continued after filling out the warrant and a short note to Fallon. "Kiowa and Zeke, if you would do the honors of taking this man to Sheriff Fallon at Hard Times, I'd appreciate it. After that, you can high tail it for home. There's probably a couple of freight wagons to unload when you get there."

He stood in front of the drovers. "Missus Pinder, what about these men? Are you going to run the ranch, or sell it?"

"I'd prefer to keep it going. I don't know what else I'd do. I've talked to Irma and she will come and stay with me. This old house is about worn out. If I can find the money Dave got from the latest cattle sale, we should be able to make payroll for quite some time."

Roundy had been hanging back watching the proceedings. When she said that, he stepped forward. "I got most of it right here, Missus Pinder. We spent some of it riding around the country. Finding Quin was like chasing smoke."

"Wait a minute." Quin put his hands on his hips. "You had all that money and still took my last forty dollars to stand drinks for your crew?"

"That's why we still have money." Roundy said smugly.

Shaking his head, he looked at the Pinder riders. "So, what about it. You going to ride for Missus Pinder?"

The man who'd spoken inside the house said. "If she'll have us. We never got the straight story on what happened to Miss Pinder or when you were shot. We just followed orders. We'll stay at least until she gets the ranch going again. That's a promise."

Maria spoke up from the porch. "I'll keep them on. Maybe next time they'll pay more attention to orders. Who knows, I may be the next one to go crazy."

"Well, I think that takes care of everything." Quin stood by Red and put everything back into his saddlebag. "Roundy, you can take charge of getting the ladies loaded up and all of you moved to the C-P Connected. Kiowa, you and Zeke can take care of Pinder. That should take care of everything. I'll just...."

"Kiowa, saddle my horse!" Connie's voice rapped out in full strength as she strode from the house.

The sudden noise made Red crow-hop a couple of times with Quin trying to hang on to the pommel.

"Well, she's back." Kiowa laughed, watching Quin dusting himself off from where he'd been dumped.

Connie glanced around and said, "I'll be leaving with Quinlan, if he'll quit falling off his horse."

Chapter Twenty-Seven

Later, after everyone had left, Connie walked to her horse. "So, you ready to go home?"

Home? Was he? With those few words, they seemed headed toward a certain union. That he wasn't fighting it was surprising. But the day had been full of surprises.

He nodded to her. "I'm glad you're coming with me."

She dusted off her skirt and mounted. "I decided I'd felt sorry for myself long enough. Well, mother told me that...and Irma. She told me that too. They also pointed out to me that if I wanted to remain alive, I needed to start living."

While sounding simple, he knew that would be the hardest thing for her to do. Getting on with life after her assault would be tedious. His reply was guarded. "Sounds like good advice."

Sighing, her gaze was worried. "I may regress sometimes and be hard to live with."

He chuckled. "You should see some of the streams near your new home. Gonna be great fishing."

"You'd run away from a woman in a bad mood?" Her voice was full of mock concern.

"Like a quail off the nest." He nodded seriously, a slow grin starting as they looked at each other.

~ * ~

They were a mile down the trail when she started. "I have a couple of questions."

His hat came off in his hands. He was back to a medium-brimmed Stetson, cavalry style, band already darkened with sweat. "Do you like this hat? You didn't think much of my last one."

"Seems like a lifetime ago, doesn't it? Do you think we'll ever see another dance?" She shook her head, smiling at him. "I'm not going to be sidetracked. We need to have a conversation...well, several. I still don't know you all that well."

With his fingers tapping the butt of his pistol, he finally sighed and gave in. Her eyebrow raised as she watched his hand. "Alright." He said with a smile. "Fire away."

"Did you really think we'd just start a new life together without some conversation?" She smirked at him a moment. "Is your real name Quinlan Barrett?"

"Actually Quinlan James Barrett, but yes, it is."

Her voice was tremulous. "Will you marry me someday, Quinlan James Barrett?"

Giving her a long look, he smiled. "Why, yes. Since you asked, yes I will."

"Uh, huh." She looked behind at the small dust trail they were leaving. "You say that, but we're going in the wrong direction, don't you think? All the preachers I know of are back there."

"We have things to take care of. You need time to heal. Hell, after a few weeks you might not like me at all and rescind the offer." He rubbed the scar on Red's mane as their horses walked an unhurried trail. Red seemed to like that. "I've a strange bunch of friends. You may not like that, either."

"You mean because they're from the tribes? And Zeke and Mattie don't exactly look like French creole?" Her chuckle turned into a full out laugh.

"Yeah, something like that. And the small fact that I've killed a lot of men lately."

"Not a factor." She said. "If the memories haunt you, I'll hold you tight until they go away. Did you know I'm adopted and part Indian, maybe full blood?"

He shrugged while giving her a look, up and down. "I'm part English. Likely we can both live it down."

Her laugh startled Red and Satan, both giving snorts and warning looks as they turned their heads. After a moment, she regained momentum. "You were born east of here?"

"Over near Elk Horn Tavern, in Arkansas. I haven't been that way in a long time. We should visit someday."

She reached in her saddlebag and pulled out a sheet of paper. "Quinlan, since you fell off your horse in our barn lot, I seem to have misjudged you at every turn. Or you deceived me. Maybe some of both. That sound about right?"

"Kinda works both ways." He gave her an amused look before scanning the brush and rocks around them. One crisis being over didn't mean there wasn't another on the horizon.

She wore a divided skirt so she could hook a leg around her saddle horn—made it kind of a side-saddle. Seemed she had a list of questions—even a pencil. "Now. You told me that dime novel you've been reading was numbered a hundred thirty-nine—those Frank Starr novels?"

He gave her a wary look. With a memory like she possessed, he'd have to be real careful with the things he said.

Snapping the list straight, she smoothed the paper out on her leg. "Well, it just so happens I got a list from the mercantile of all those books. Sadie was very helpful with that. She likes to read, too."

"When did you get that list?"

"Well, it was before the dance and all the troubles. But it's no less important now. Did you know we can order them? Now, I figure you're on this list somewhere between number one and a hundred thirty-eight. And we are for damned-sure going to find out which story is about you before we get home."

She gave him a sweet smile. "And don't worry, we have all night."

"I don't plan on us talking all night." He said mildly.

Stiffening in the saddle, she said softly. "It's too soon for that, Quinlan."

It was his turn to smile. "Wasn't talking about that. I value my sleep."

She relaxed, smoothing the paper against her leg. "That's fine, Quinlan. You need to get your rest because your world is about to change."

The soft, shuffling hoofbeats hardly broke through the evening serenity as they pointed their horses toward the campsite and spring they'd stayed at before.

Tomorrow they'd make an easy ride into Spring Valley and home.

The End

~ * ~ * ~ * ~

Thank you for reading. Sounds trite, but many people don't. This isn't about me. You are the person reading my stories. So, thank you for taking the time and hopefully take a little history with you when you've finished. Check out my website and rummage around awhile. You're welcome to escape into my stories anytime you like. Comments are always welcome.

Darrel Sparkman

~ * ~ * ~ * ~

Darrel Sparkman, Author

... a noble race but they are gone
with their old forests wide and deep,
and we have built our homes upon
fields where their generations sleep.

~ William Cullen Bryant, 1878

Darrel Sparkman is an award-winning author of novels, novellas, and short stories. A recent recipient of the prestigious Will Rogers Medallion Award, he's been included in three western anthologies. This author also worked as a feature writer for Saddlebag Dispatches and blogger for Sundown Press. Ideas come from a diverse past of serving as a combat search and rescue helicopter crewman in Vietnam and volunteer Emergency Medical Technician First Responder. He has worked as a professional photographer, in computer repair and was part-owner of a commercial greenhouse operation and flower shop.

Darrel is enjoying semi-retirement and finally has that job that wakes you up every day with a smile.

Note from Darrel

I never studied much; school wasn't a big interest for me. In retrospect, I wish I had. But what I did was read. Didn't have much of a childhood, so I read to escape, four to five books a week—from middle school into adulthood. You name it—I read it.

Being raised in rural America bent me toward adventure novels and westerns. Reading an adventure novel and wanting to get on to the next one gave me the style in my writing of picking a week or so in the protagonist's life and riding hell-bent from problem to solution. My heroes are prone to suddenness of action and intent.

Writing can exorcise your demons, give you the pleasure of a story well told, and drive you to distraction. But it is always a ride worth taking.

See more at:
http://darrelsparkman.com
http://facebook.com/DarrelSparkman.author
http://amazon.com/author/darrelsparkman